THE LADY OF CLAN MACKINLAY

BETA COPY

HIGHLAND LOVERS

CECELIA MECCA

THE LADY OF CLAN MACKINLAY

CHAPTER ONE

Duncraig Castle, Scottish Highlands, 13th century

"The Duncraig wishes to see you both."

Niall all but laughed in his clansman's face. He and his brother Kieran had been training, as they did most days, when their father's friend found them. Dougal and their father had been raised together, and though most thought the two cousins, they were, in fact, naught but clansmen.

"Wishes?" Kieran asked the question Niall had been about to raise. When did their father ever wish for anything? Chief of Clan Duncraig for more than twenty years, he commanded. Demanded. But he never "wished" for aught to happen. Including summoning his sons.

Dougal shrugged. "Seemed a kinder message than the one he gave."

Niall and Kieran exchanged a glance.

"Go on then," Niall said, sheathing his claymore as Kieran did the same. "Give us the message."

Poor Dougal looked uncomfortable now. But since Niall and Kieran loved nothing more than making Dougal squirm, for no other reason than he did so much too easily, neither man budged. Known as the "Rock of Duncraig" for his apparent lack of emotion, Niall would never reveal his inner thoughts. His brother, however, very well may burst into laughter at any moment.

Niall gave him a look that said, *Do not. Let this play out.*

Poor Dougal.

He shifted from one foot to the other. How this man was the same one who saved their father's life on the battlefield, who was as close to the chief of Clan Duncraig as any man, but was still half-afraid of him, almost made Niall smile.

Almost.

"He said to come to the keep," Dougal said, turning as if to walk away from them.

Niall shook his head as his brother began to follow. Kieran rolled his eyes.

Niall may be a right bastard. A coldhearted warrior through and through. A "stubborn goat like your father," according to their mother. But if he loved one thing besides his family and clan, it was a jest. And this one was too good to pass on. Making Dougal repeat their father's foul-mouthed demand—since there was no doubt that was the reason Dougal hesitated—was nearly as much fun as having his brother yield to him.

"Ah." Dougal turned back to them. Framed by lush green mountains and the familiar silhouette of Castle Duncraig on the hill behind him, Dougal made a right sight. Niall struggled to keep a smile from his face. "You'll make me say it?"

"Aye," his brother said, clearly impatient to be on his way. Unlike Niall, Kieran's primary concern was always pleasing their father. Mayhap because Niall seemed to do it more naturally, he never actively attempted as much. If his father did not care for his temperament, or mannerisms, or decisions, the chief would let him know. And Niall may or may not change course.

Kieran? He would do anything for their father's approval.

"You know I do nae cuss, lad."

"I know it well," Niall said. 'Twas an oddity that could not be found among any other Duncraig clansman. "But 'tis the chief's words, not your own."

"Aye," his brother added. "If anything, the Duncraig is liable for giving you such a message knowing your dislike for such language."

Dougal gave them both such a look.

The man loved them like sons too. As he had none of his own, they only did their duty to treat him as they would family. And in their family, none went a day without a gentle provoking.

"Your father," Dougal said, likely knowing the chief would not be pleased at the delay, "bid me to fetch 'my two blethering neds' from the training yard."

"Hmm," Niall's brother said, "'tis not so bad. I'd say he's spot-on describing Niall. Sorry, brother, but you're more of an instigator than any I know."

"Perhaps," he said. "But if he meant either of us blethered, 'tis easily you. Though I will admit, you've done less of it today than usual."

As the two of them continued to trade barbs, Dougal shook his head, made an indistinguishable sound, and left them. Finally allowing himself to smile as his back was turned, he noticed Kieran did the same. The brothers began to follow Dougal continuing all the way up the hill, through the courtyard, and into the keep.

It was only when they entered the mostly empty great hall and saw their father's expression that the brothers quickly desisted from their antics.

The Duncraig, as he was widely known, was not angry.

He was furious.

Their father did not get red in the face over a delay. This had naught to do with them, a fact he confirmed as both Kieran and Niall approached him.

"When have you last seen him this angry?" Kieran whispered.

Niall did not answer. Could not, as they were now within earshot of him. But the answer, had he given it, would have been, "Not in a long, long time."

"MacKinlay."

'Twas just one word. But enough to understand at least part of his anger. They feuded with many clans, but none as fiercely as Clan MacKinlay. The king of Scotland himself had been forced to intervene some fifteen years ago. Back then, thirty of Duncraig's men had fought thirty of MacKinlay's, and though Duncraig saw losses, the fight had not ended until every one of MacKinley's warriors, including their chief, lay dead, effectively ending a decades-long feud. Since the Battle of The Black Friars, the word "MacKinlay" was all but banned in these halls.

"What have they done?" Kieran asked. Even Dougal looked surprised. Clearly he did not know why they'd been fetched. If any of them had, they'd not have wasted time coming to the hall.

"Their cattle were found grazing on our land along the northern border."

Shite.

Fifteen years. And now this. 'Twas enough to bring

another war between their clans, as every man in this hall well knew.

"You will go to their chief and put a stop to it," their father said, though not clarifying which of them would do so.

"Should you not go as chief?" Niall asked the obvious question.

Their father's grimace was his answer. For a moment, Niall thought 'twould be the only one. But then he ground out, "If I go there, I will kill him. And we will be at war once again."

CHAPTER

TWO

"Again."

"You've hit every mark, my lady."

"Nay," Avelina said to her brother's squire. She, of course, as a woman, had no squire. But neither that, nor the fact that she was, indeed, a woman, stopped her from training with the bow she'd learned to use many years ago. "That second one missed its mark."

"Most men cannae come close to the bullseye line, my lady. That you've hit it with your worst shot, and that the meal is surely nearly finished by now—"

"Again," Avelina said more firmly. And then added, "If you please."

She was no tyrant, and as Callum fetched her arrows, she realized he was likely hungry, having been with her much of the afternoon. The training yard had emptied long ago, and so when he returned, Avelina took the arrows and told him to leave.

"Go to the meal. I will be along," she said.

He looked hesitant. For good reason. Avelina's brother, the chief, had given the boy of ten and five a most ridiculous task. Not to leave her side during training.

Helpful at times? Aye. But since the training yard was located within the outer walls of the castle, there was no reason for such a precaution. Did Ewan believe their castle walls would be breached at any moment, putting her in danger? She'd asked him that question many times, always to be given the same answer.

"The training yard, alone, is no place for a woman."

Which made little sense. In fact, as she landed all four arrows directly in the center this time, gathered her bows, and made her way back to the keep, Avelina decided to speak with Ewan. Without changing gowns, she did precisely that, sitting next to him on the dais.

"I've saved you a pear tart," he said, the meal having been presented already. When one of the servants asked what she wished for him to bring, Avelina moved the pear tart toward her.

"This shall be all," she said.

The servant looked at her oddly, and Ewan asked what the maid would not. "You will eat a pear tart as your meal?"

With more than thirty men, and some women, eating in the hall with them, Ewan had been forced to raise his voice to be heard. The weather had improved of late, making for a rowdier bunch than usual.

'Twas the opening she needed.

"On the morrow," she speculated as her wine goblet was filled, "is it not possible I could be in the training yard when I am suddenly attacked? Or even killed?" *To think my last meal might have been a pear tart.* "What a sweet idea indeed."

Ewan, accustomed to her and her antics, did not hesitate. "I regret to inform you, sister dear, if that were to indeed occur, your last meal would likely have been fresh bread or perhaps porridge. Or do you not plan to break your fast on the morrow so that this"—he indicated the tart Avelina currently ate—"will be your last meal?"

She had not thought of that.

"You are many things," Ewan said, taking a sip of wine as was his custom at the evening meal. All other times, 'twas ale for him. "Fiery. Brave. A skilled archer. But cleverer than me?" He shrugged as if to say, nay, she was not that.

"I disagree." Avelina thought back not very far into the past to present her case. "Less than a sennight ago, when you could not determine the cause of the smell in the east tower—"

"I did not try overly hard before you discovered the rotten piece of meat."

"I was told you had been looking all morn for the source."

He did not comment, so she added, "But since I know Whitefoot's habits better than you..."

"Since you cannot be parted with him," Ewan said. "Some would think him your child and not merely a dog by how you treat him."

"Do not disparage my bairn," she teased.

"Jest all you wish, but you came to the hall annoyed with me," he countered. "I would know the reason."

Ewan had been the most observant man in the room for as long as she could remember. Perhaps it was because he'd been forced to lead at such a young age. The Battle of The Black Friars had taken thirty of Clan MacKinlay's men in one battle those many years ago—their father, their uncles, and nearly all who would have been named chief losing their lives in one fell swoop. At ten and six, Ewan had become the youngest chief of their clan.

For years her brother had been appointed guardians, who called themselves the provisional chiefs of their clan until Ewan came of age. But that age was still far too young in Avelina's opinion. His childhood taken from him, her brother had always served more as a father to her, and these times when he could tease her, like a brother might, were ones she cherished.

But the chief was back.

She sighed. "You know already. Your silly decree—"

"'Tis not silly, Sister."

"So you believe."

"So I know."

"My opinion matters little?"

"Do not attribute words to me I did not utter, Lina."

She was about to respond when their cousin Fergus burst into the hall. Avelina wasn't sure why their clansman was not at the meal, as he lived with his wife in Castle MacKinlay, serving as her brother's second. The man was never far from Ewan.

"I must speak with you, Chief," he said, the formal address due to others being present. "Immediately."

"Come." Ewan motioned him closer. "You may do so here."

Fergus gave Avelina a quick nod, acknowledging her presence and Ewan's willingness to receive the message with her present. For all his faults, her brother did not typically leave her in the dark. As nothing more than the chief's sister, she was aware this was not always the case.

"There are rumors."

Avelina had never in all her life seen Fergus look as he did now. The man's deep auburn beard hid much of his face, but 'twas plain to see in his eyes, their poor cousin was concerned.

"Tell me," her brother said, his voice hard.

"A merchant just arrived from the village. Said a pair of riders wearing the Duncraig plaid were seen coming through."

Avelina whipped her head toward her brother. Though the weather had improved of late, summer approaching fast, a shiver ran through her as if a cold blast of air had just invaded their keep. Avelina actually hugged herself as if to keep warm.

"Impossible."

Fergus swallowed. "I found and spoke with the merchant myself. He is just outside the keep. And is certain. The man has been alive long enough to know the Duncraig plaid even if it's not been seen around these parts for many years."

"So you are saying he is old?"

"Aye."

Her brother had little patience with anything but directness. "Say as much, Cousin."

"I will tell you then, 'tis them."

"Coming here?"

"Appears so, aye."

As her brother said, 'twas impossible. "They'd never do such a thing," she blurted. "Nay. Not possible."

Their oldest enemies, Clan Duncraig, had all but decimated Clan MacKinlay. 'Twas only by the sheer will of the women who remained behind to forge alliances to keep them safe that they had survived. The next generation, including her brother, had led the regrowth that made Clan MacKinlay a force to be reckoned with once again.

From the ashes.

The new clan motto they'd adopted nigh five years ago. In all this time, not once had a Duncraig dared come near their land. Neither had MacKinlay clansmen tempted fate by finding themselves within two days' ride of Clan Duncraig's land. If there was a meeting of the clans and either were to attend, the other held back.

"'Tis exceedingly odd," her brother mused.

Nay, more than odd. "'Tis an outrage. Do they believe they can simply ride through the gates of our castle unbidden? As if we would allow them entry."

Her brother nodded, seemingly agreeing with her. "I cannae think they mean to gain entry, but we will go nonetheless." He stood. "To be certain."

As if expecting as much, Fergus already stepped away from the dais and began to head to the hall's entrance.

Avelina would not be dissuaded from accompanying them. When Ewan looked at her as if to say, "You should remain here," Avelina preempted him with, "You will have to pin me down screaming to keep me behind."

A prospect, it seemed, Ewan did not relish. Shaking his head, he followed Fergus and Avelina followed both men.

Partly infuriated at the audacity of these Duncraig clansmen and partly curious, she lifted the hem of her gown to catch up with Ewan and Fergus. Even worse, she cursed the newcomers in her head, for she'd had only a few bites of her pear tart. As if she needed another reason to resent the most unwelcome intrusion Castle MacKinlay had ever seen in her lifetime.

'Twas an interesting turn of events she could never have predicted.

Duncraig clansmen. Here. She had to see evidence of it to believe it.

CHAPTER
THREE

"Through the village. A worthy idea, Brother," Niall said as they rode toward the keep, no less than two dozen horsemen at their back by now.

If his brother reached down between his legs, Niall was certain Kieran would not be able to grasp his own bawsack. It was that large. Some may even call him reckless, but secretly, when he wasn't on the precipice of getting himself killed.

"Should we have snuck in then? Finding ourselves with backs full of arrows?"

"Perhaps circumnavigating the village may have been advantageous," Niall responded, knowing full well Kieran had understood his meaning the first time.

His brother turned to look behind them. "They seem less than pleased."

"Perhaps as pleased as I am to be on MacKinlay land."

"And yet, thirty of your best men, including your clan's chief, were not slaughtered."

"A happy circumstance of being better-trained warriors."

"Mmmm. . ." Kieran had a surprising softness for their enemy, one Niall could never understand. He hated them, aye. Would not be here today if their father had not demanded it. And yet, when they spoke of the battle, Niall's brother often attempted to force him into considering Clan MacKinley's position. As if their clans had not been feuding for decades, forcing the king to such extreme measures as commanding the battle that had decimated Clan MacKinlay.

The two fell silent for the remainder of the ride to the gatehouse of a castle Niall had never been inside before. Once, when he was but a child, his father had taken him to the top of a mountain where Castle MacKinlay could be seen far off in the distance. He told both Niall and his brother of the feud between their clans. Spoke of alliances and enemies and the importance of knowing the difference between them even when, at times, 'twas difficult to discern. Some, like Clan MacKinlay, had always been and would always be enemies. But others may be enemies in disguise, a fleeting alliance giving way to true intentions. Knowing who to trust, he'd told Niall, would be the most difficult lesson he would learn as future chief.

"I expected hostile," his brother said now. "But not an army against two people."

As they approached the gatehouse, Niall and Kieran's decision not to take any clansmen with them—a decision their father had not agreed with—seemed perhaps foolish now. Not wanting to inflame an already inflammatory situation, they'd come alone.

Clan MacKinlay did not seem to care there were but two of them.

In addition to the thirty or so riding behind them that Niall and Kieran had picked up since the village, the gatehouse and barbican were filled with MacKinlay warriors. Where a few guards may have otherwise been stationed, there were now easily fifty men.

And, it appeared, one woman. Niall could not see her face, but high above him, standing on the castle wall, was clearly a woman among men. The lady of Castle MacKinlay, perhaps? The chief's mother had died some years ago, so either the chief was married or 'twas the sister. Clan Duncraig may not have interacted with their enemy in many years, but they knew all there was to know of MacKinlay.

"You are not welcome here" were the first words anyone said.

They came from a man, though Niall could not see which one. The words were shouted, their meaning quite clear.

"We wish to be here as heartily as you wish for us to be at your gates. But there is a matter we must discuss. I am Niall, son of the Duncraig, and this is my brother, Kieran. We seek an audience with your chief."

"I am the chief of MacKinlay," the man said. He stood directly next to the woman, though Niall could see neither of their features from this distance. "And do not wish to grant you an audience."

Niall sighed. He'd hoped this would go quickly, allowing him to spend as little time on MacKinlay property as possible.

"I fear turning us away is not a possibility," he called.

His brother sighed. Kieran would likely have phrased his response much differently. Only one of them was tactful, and he was not Niall.

"We've more than a hundred men to your two who say otherwise," the chief called. Though Niall could not see him well, he knew the chief, like him and Kieran, had not yet seen thirty years. But also like the two of them, he'd already seen plenty of battles.

"We are but two men," his peacekeeping brother called to the chief.

"Two Duncraig clansmen," the chief responded as if that was all that mattered. And perhaps it was. Still, they'd not be leaving without that audience.

"We come with a message from our chief that I mean to deliver. Allow us entry or take us prisoner so we may speak to you from behind the bars of a prison cell. Either way, we will speak to you. And if 'tis the latter, you can be certain of starting our feud anew, which is precisely what we are here to prevent."

"You speak in riddles," the chief called down. "State your business and be gone."

Goddammit.

"Our business is, as my brother said, to prevent another clan war. But we will not shout the matter up to you. We are but two men. Disarm us and allow us to enter so we may speak with you."

Silence. And then the chief did something Niall's father was rarely seen to do.

Consult with those around him.

The Duncraig made decisions unilaterally, for better or worse, and then dealt with the fallout if necessary. In a way, Niall respected his decisiveness. But it was something he'd not replicate as chief. Sometimes, others simply knew more and 'twas a wise decision to learn from them. Of course, the Duncraig had been chief for a long time. Likely his father had been more temperate at the age of the MacKinlay chief.

The silence wore on, but Niall, comfortable in it, remained stoic. He looked ahead, showed no emotion, and waited. Finally, without warning, the portcullis lifted. As it creaked open, he did finally glance at his brother.

For the first time in his life, he would enter the very pit of hell. Through those gates, to meet the men who had harassed his ancestors, kidnapped his great aunt, and caused his clan more grief than any other. Until the Battle of The Black Friars, that is.

When the gate was finally lifted and he and Kieran began to ride under it, Niall ignored the looks of the MacKinlay warriors and stared straight ahead. And now, it seemed, 'twas time to dance.

CHAPTER
FOUR

"Nay, Avelina," her brother began as he made his way down to the courtyard.

She, of course, ignored him.

Thankfully, he was too preoccupied with receiving, unbelievably, a Duncraig clansman to further harangue her. As her own clansmen gathered, attempting to push her behind them, she stood on her tiptoes, sure they must have made their way through the gatehouse by now.

Not just any Duncraig clansmen—the chief's sons.

'Twas daring coming here this way. Though her brother would never condone an unprovoked attack against two men, there were many less scrupulous clan chiefs who would not hesitate to do so, even at the risk of beginning a new clan war. Both sons came alone and apparently unarmed, if she understood the gist of what was happening.

They'd given up their weapons.

'Twas no use. She could not get through this way. Instead, Avelina went around the gathered men to the other side, an impenetrable circle seemingly having been formed.

Dammit. There were so many times, this one included, that Avelina rued the day she'd been born a woman and not a man.

A man would use his brute strength to push through. And though she was not as strong as any of those gathered before her, perhaps 'twas their boldness that mattered just as much. And so, instead of gently pushing on the backs of her clansmen, Avelina pretended she were one of them, and without hesitation, pushed with all her might. Sure enough, though the odd looks she received told her they were taken aback, Avelina was able to push through to the front of the circle.

She finally could both see and hear what was happening at the same time.

"We would speak to you alone," the handsome one said to her brother.

Nay, they were both handsome. And large. And fearsome looking. But the one who spoke to Ewan now had a look about him that Avelina could not tear her gaze from. Unrelenting. Intense. He stared down her brother as if Ewan were not the powerful clan chief he'd become. As if not even the king of Scotland himself would intimidate him. His brown hair curled in the most magnificent ways to and fro. Squarish cheekbones. Chin held high. A stance that defied the odds, given he and his brother were surrounded on all sides.

But of all that captivated her about him, 'twas his voice that most penetrated her very core. 'Twas deep and strong. Deliberate, and dare she think it, as sensual a voice as Avelina had ever heard before.

"You asked for an audience and have one. Speak your piece, Duncraig."

"Alone," was the only word he spoke.

Fergus stepped closer to her brother. The circle of men became impatient. Aye, these men were her enemy. Her greatest enemies, in fact, for it was their clan that had taken her father, her grandfather, two of Avelina's uncles...

And yet, for all of that, and for her desire to train with a bow, there was one thing Avelina despised above all. Bloodshed.

As a girl, she'd vomited the first time she saw her brother injured. Her aversion to blood did not begin and end with humans either. When an animal was injured, even for the sake of becoming food that sustained her family and clan, Avelina could not witness it. She even attempted, for a time, not to eat anything that could be killed, but she'd grown so sick that her brother forced her to eat rabbit for every meal for days until the color had come back to her cheeks.

The fear that blood might be drawn in front of her—even if it were of these men who deserved nothing less than quick deaths for their clan's role in the demise of her family—spurred Avelina.

"This is not an audience," she said, speaking clearly and stepping into the circle. She might not be chief, but she was the sister of the chief. Daughter of the late chief. And the only woman present. Sometimes Avelina wondered what she and her fellow sisterhood of women could do if only they were allowed to rule as the men did. Likely, there would be less war. "'Tis an assailment."

Every single man present, including the Duncraig clansmen, turned to her. Looked at her.

He looked at her.

Avelina had no notion of what she'd been about to say. Every thought, every intention, simply vanished. She was certain her brother was also looking at her, murderously no doubt, but she could not validate the thought. Because she locked eyes with a pair the color of the sky. On a sunny day. Light blue. A shade Avelina was certain she'd never seen before. Yet somehow, even though they were such a bright, vibrant color, his gaze was anything but friendly.

"Lady Avelina," her brother said, breaking the spell.

Indeed, if he used her title, he was vexed with her. She reluctantly looked his way. Arguing with the chief in front of others would earn her ears a severe lecture. But she cared not.

"If they were any other men—"

"They are not," Ewan said, the word "not" with an emphasis none could mistake, "any other men. We will treat here or not at all."

She would try one final time. But before she could say anything, the Duncraig chief's son spoke up. "MacKinlay cattle were found grazing on Duncraig land along the northern border." He said that looking at her but now turned his attention to Ewan.

"Impossible. Our lands do not border. They would have had to be led there through Tannochbrae land."

Everyone began speaking at once. Nay, shouting. All saying the same thing. That unless someone wished to start a war anew with their clans, 'twas impossible for their cattle to be so far southeast. As they spoke, Avelina once again caught the gaze of chief's second. This time, he appeared slightly less hostile. And even perhaps. . . appreciative. Of her intervention? Or something else?

She'd been called beautiful many times. Avelina's opinion of herself was of a pretty woman who could perhaps be more so if she chose to wear rouge on her cheeks or spent the time necessary to pile her hair atop her head in the latest style. Instead, she was what her brother often referred to as... wild. Untamed.

She took a step toward the chief's second.

He did the same.

Without notice, they came together until Avelina was so close to him if he reached out to grab her, the man could do so easily. She opened her mouth, unsure what was to come out... and Ewan suddenly reached out to grab her, pulling her behind him. Though she struggled to free her arm, he would not relent.

"Your recklessness will get you killed, Lina," he whispered harshly. As harshly as she'd ever heard her brother speak to her. 'Twas likely the presence of these Duncraig clansmen, but still, she liked it not.

"Invite them into the keep," she said. "Surely you need the full story of the news they bring. If 'tis indeed true—"

But he'd stopped listening. She sighed, once again catching the eyes of the chief's second.

This time his expression seemed almost amused. He did not smile, per se, but something about the twinkle in his eyes gave her that impression.

As the crowd continued discussing, loudly, the impact of the Duncraig's words reverberating through the circle, her brother finally called for an end to it.

"You will both follow me."

And just like that, 'twas done. The circle parted for their chief. The newcomers followed Ewan, neither of them looking her way as they passed, and it seemed for the first time in Avelina's lifetime, the keep of Castle MacKinlay would welcome clansmen from Duncraig.

Although "welcome" may not be the correct word to use, they were headed in the keep's direction. Swordless, though still proud, they followed her brother. And Avelina had no intention of missing this meeting, so she sped along as well.

Not for another glimpse of the Duncraig warrior, but simply because she'd not be denied the opportunity for some excitement. And of one thing there was no doubt, today was proving to be the most exciting day that Avelina could recall in a long, long time.

CHAPTER
FIVE

Niall couldn't see her any longer. But he could feel her presence behind him as they entered the hall. Clan MacKinlay crests everywhere, the hall similar in size to their own, the air more oppressive with every step... 'twas a feeling he could not put words to. He did not care for being here, in a place he'd heard so much about, none of it good.

"I would offer for you to break your fast," the chief said, "but we've done so already."

And they would not choose to break their fast with them either way. That part was left unsaid, but 'twas just as well. He and his brother had no wish to remain any longer than necessary.

The chief of MacKinlay made his way to the dais. Niall turned to look and found only about seven or eight warriors had followed, likely members of the clan council. And her.

Lady Avelina. A fitting name, as beautiful as the woman herself. Light brown hair, unbound. Brown eyes, as deep as they were bright. Cheeks he would dearly love to grab with both hands as he held her head firmly before kissing her.

She was unmarried, but Niall knew little else about her. Except, of course, that he should not be thinking of the chief of MacKinlay's sister in such a way.

There she was.

Lady Avelina followed her brother up onto the dais, where three chairs were positioned facing them. No table, as it had likely been taken away after the meal. As the other MacKinlay warriors gathered, the chief, Lady Avelina, and another man all took their seats.

He tore his gaze from the woman who had intervened on their behalf for reasons he could only speculate about and focused instead on the man to the chief's left.

"My second," MacKinlay said by way of introductions. "Tell me about these cattle."

Niall ignored the angry glares all around them.

"We received word, as I said, that MacKinlay cattle were found grazing on Duncraig land along the northern border. Before coming here, my brother and I verified the fact." He pointed behind the chief's head toward the crest on a tapestry that hung high on the stone wall. "That was the brand, or a simplified version of it, we found on nearly two dozen of the cattle openly grazing there."

"On the northern border of your land?"

His skepticism was warranted, but unwelcome.

"Aye," his brother said, likely sensing Niall's irritation.

"You questioned Mackenzie?" the chief asked.

"Of course," he said, to the chief's irritation. But Niall had not come here to coddle the man. He came here for answers. "Would you care to tell us why, then?"

As MacKinlay exchanged a glance with his second, Niall snuck a peek at the woman. She was watching him. Nay, staring at him. Boldly. Something told him 'twas her way, that Lady Avelina was as intimate with boldness as he was with rarely showing emotion—something his mother complained about endlessly as if doing so might change him.

"Why our cattle grazed on your land? 'Tis simple. They did not," the second, Fergus, said.

Niall would not let that stand. "You call my brother and me liars? We saw the brand ourselves." His raised voice echoed through the hall. Tensions, which had already been high, remained so.

"I say no MacKinlay would do such a thing," Fergus continued. "We've avoided another war with your clan for fifteen years. Why would we provoke one now?"

"That is the question," Niall's more temperate brother said, "we are here to answer."

None spoke immediately, and Niall took the opportunity to peek again at the sister. Still, she looked at him.

Bold, my lady, are we not?

She seemed to defy any judgment his silent question held. Though, in truth, it held none. Niall had never seriously entertained marriage, knowing eventually he must. But when he did think of the type of woman who he'd wish by his side for a lifetime, it would certainly be one more like his mother than his Aunt Margaret, who spent her days nodding in agreement with his uncle even when he acted like an arse.

Of course, neither would it be a woman who was his bitter enemy, but there was no doubt Lady Avelina intrigued him.

"It seems we will not solve this so easily," Lady Avelina said. Clearly, the sister held a certain position in the clan, and with her brother, to speak so freely. Even if that same brother did appear more than a bit annoyed with her interference. Though he said naught to stop her. "Shall we go, then? To see these cattle?"

Every man in the hall turned their attention to Lady Avelina. For her part, the sister seemed unbothered even if some of the looks were less than friendly. Fergus, for instance, glared at her as if she'd suggested the two clans become allies and not journey two days together. Though Niall did not relish the idea of being in MacKinlay's presence for so long, 'twas not a bad idea.

"We can leave immediately," he said. "Despite it, we cannot guarantee the cattle will still be there."

"Ach," Fergus said, "of course you cannae."

"Enough," the chief said. He locked eyes with Niall.

The hate coming from him was understandable, and Niall could not deny a measure of his own. He'd been raised to believe there was nothing closer to hell than a MacKinlay clansman. And yet, Lady Avelina looked to him more like an angel than the devil incarnate.

"You would be amenable to this plan?" MacKinlay asked him.

With a quick glance at his brother, Niall answered, "Aye."

As decisive as Niall had seen him, MacKinlay stood up. "I will summon the kitchen to offer you a meal. And then we leave immediately."

"We've as little wish to remain here the eve as your guest," Niall said, "as you do to host us. But surely you'd prefer to wait until morn. There was an inn in the village—"

"Every moment we delay is another the cattle may stray."

"A true enough fact," Kieran said.

"We shall leave at once. You've two men. We will bring the same number." Ewan turned to Fergus, who nodded.

"Fair enough," Niall said.

Then the three words were spoken that he'd secretly wished to hear and also dreaded.

Lady Avelina said, "I am coming."

CHAPTER SIX

"Quickly," she said to her lady's maid.

Mary had come to her years ago as the daughter of a poor family from the village. They'd met at the blacksmith's shop, and at the time, Avelina had no maid. When her mother died the year after their father and so many other MacKinlay men were slain in the Battle of the Black Friars, Avelina had chosen not to need anyone. Not a maid. Not a husband, which her brother had attempted to secure for her in the years since. Not knowing if they might stay or leave, she wished to rely on none, hence her insistence on learning to wield a bow and arrow.

Though they'd never met before, when she and Mary first shared a space in the corner of the blacksmith's shop—Avelina to speak with the man on her brother's behalf, Mary to procure nails from the smith—there had been a connection between them immediately. One she could not explain then, nor now, but that mattered little.

Now that Mary was married with a wee bairn, her duties had shifted slightly, and sometimes, Avelina could admit to herself, she missed the closeness they'd shared. 'Twas not the same since Mary had met her now-husband, but Avelina had come to accept the fact. Mostly.

"If they left without you, 'twould be a blessing, methinks."

As Mary prepared her satchel, Avelina finished tying her boots. She'd changed into a riding gown, its deep green able to hide the marks that would come inevitably with travel.

"I would not miss it for the world. 'Tis the most exciting thing to happen in as long as I can remember."

"More exciting than Alistair's visit?"

Alistair. The most serious of her suitors and the only one Avelina was truly considering. His clan was an ally of MacKinlay. He was handsome. Kind. There was nothing that did not recommend the man as a potential husband. Except...

"Aye," she admitted. "My heart has never leapt looking at him as it did today."

Mary sighed. "With the chief's son."

As if they would be talking about any other. When Avelina had found Mary after her brother decreed they would leave soon, very reluctantly agreeing for her to come, she'd told her everything. Of course, the maid already knew there were Duncraig clansmen in their keep. But she'd been more than a little surprised by the news Avelina carried. Mary had expected distaste, and anger, and of course, Avelina held both in her heart for the two men, but she could also not deny her body's response.

It was the same as in the courtyard but more so. Every time they exchanged a glance...

Except, she hated him. She hated him, his brother, his family, his clan. If only someone would inform her stupid heart of the fact so that it may beat normally again in his presence.

"Aye," she admitted. "'Tis wrong. I know it to be so. Of course, I hate the man."

Mary handed Avelina the satchel. "As you should."

"I do."

"'Tis well."

"Aye, very well."

The women's eyes locked. Mary sighed. "My lady. Do not. He can never be yours."

"I do not wish him to be mine."

Lie.

"And yet, your eyes sparkle with anticipation."

"To go on an adventure."

"With the Duncraig clansman."

"He will be there, aye."

Mary rolled her eyes. "Listen to me well. You claim to hate the man, but those are merely words coming from your mouth. I believe you want to hate him but realize he was just a young man, as you were a young woman, when the Battle of the Black Friars occurred. You know he is as much to blame as me, and because of it, you allow the possibility that he is not a bad man. One you are clearly attracted to."

As always, Mary's insight was keen.

"I hate the man," she insisted.

"And like him too. But you must know, he can never be yours. Your brother would never, ever, agree to a match with a Duncraig."

"Nor should he," Avelina agreed.

"Nor should he." Mary sighed. "Now go before they leave you."

Avelina gave her maid, her friend, a quick hug, and

knowing she was right—'twas very possible they might leave her behind—Avelina sped through the corridors back to the hall. Indeed, 'twas empty.

Avelina made her way into the courtyard and breathed a sigh of relief spotting the riding party apparently waiting for her. Attaching her satchel and mounting her palfrey, Avelina avoided *his* gaze. One that had been on her from the moment she stepped into the courtyard.

The sight of MacKinlay and Duncraig clansmen riding alongside one another caused quite a stir. Indeed, 'twas not until they were well past the village that the five riders were not the subject of curious stares.

I want to speak to him.

She should not want that. And was unsure how to facilitate it with the chief's son and his brother well ahead of her, Ewan, and Fergus. There was no way to do such a thing. Or so she thought. Until, a short time later, the chief's second fell back to speak to her brother briefly. She could not hear their conversation, but Avelina did speed up her mount to ride on the other side of the Duncraig warrior.

He caught her eye. And, apparently finished with her brother, allowed the others to ride ahead so the two of them remained in the back.

"Did you wish to speak with me?" he asked, his voice low, cutting through her chest, and other parts of her, in a way no other voice had.

Avelina could never be confused with a shy maid and would not be so now. "Aye."

"What of, my lady?"

He spoke to her much more cordially or, at least, with less hostility than he did her brother.

A fine question, but one she should not answer. *Of anything* did not seem appropriate.

"Of the cattle," she heard herself blurt. Cattle. As if Avelina truly wished to speak of cattle.

"Cattle," he repeated.

"Aye."

He waited.

She cleared her throat. "I believe you," she said, sincere. "But also know 'tis impossible for them to have found their way to your land on their own."

"Agreed, my lady."

Absurdly, Avelina wanted him to say her name. They were strangers. And enemies. Yet, she wished it anyway. Life was precious, and so, she asked for what she wished. "You may call me by my given name." Avelina struggled to think of a reason why she would allow such a thing. "We journey together," she said finally. "Should not we be on familiar terms?"

It was an absurd reason, and they likely both knew it.

"Aye," he said, surprising her. "We should. Avelina."

It was as pleasing a sound as she imagined it would be. But Avelina was not yet finished. "Lina," she said. "'Tis what most call me." Which was not true. Her family and close friends called her that, but she wanted to hear it from his lips.

"Lina," he said with a half smile.

If she'd thought him handsome before...

"I am Niall. No shortened name to speak of."

The corners of her lips tugged upward. "Niall."

Whatever was between them should not be. Avelina was as aware of that fact as she was of the warrior who rode beside her. Yet, she seemed unable to stop herself.

"So, do you believe, Niall—"

He smiled. Blessed be the Virgin Mary, that smile...

"Do I believe?"

What had she been saying? Oh, aye, she remembered. "Do you believe someone led them there apurpose?"

"I do."

"One of our clansmen?"

"Perhaps."

Avelina thought on that for a moment. "Who else but the owner of the cattle would lead them away from their lands?"

"That is, indeed, a question I hope to answer. If your brother can identify their owner, perhaps we can ask him that very question."

"Or her?"

"Do you have many women in your clan who own cattle outright, then?"

"We do. Since many of our men were brutally murdered some ten and five years ago."

If she thought to get a rise out of him, Avelina was to be disappointed.

"I would not use the word 'murder,' my lady. Lina," he corrected himself.

It was much too intimate. She should have never given him leave to use that name. But, as she suspected, there was a sort of pleasure that came from hearing the sound that made her want to ask him to say it again.

She didn't, of course.

"What word would you use, Niall?"

His tongue flicked out so quickly she almost missed it, first touching his upper lip, then the lower. She wished to see that tongue again.

Lina, in the name of your Lord in heaven. What is wrong with you?

"Killed. The battle was sanctioned and attended by the

king and agreed to on both sides. Murder implies otherwise."

While she thought of how to respond, Niall continued, "I am sorry for your loss, my. . . Lina. I'd not wish what you endured on my worst enemy."

"Your worst enemy. Meaning me?"

"Your clan, aye. Not you."

"I am my clan."

He had no response to that. They fell silent.

"I was at the keep," she said finally, "when the spectators, including my mother, returned. I remember little but the weeping. And later, the fresh graves, so many of them. Oddly, though, I cannot remember aught else about that day or the ones that followed. Of course, I felt the absence of my father, my uncle, my clansmen—but of that day? Very little."

"A horror none should have to endure. Your mind protects you from it by not remembering."

Again, they fell into silence. And though she wished to continue speaking to him, Avelina said nothing more. They were not two people from opposing clans attempting to conduct a conversation. They were the son and daughter of a decades-long feud, one that had resulted in bloodshed of the sort that nearly wiped out the entirety of her clan.

Nay, Niall was not just an enemy. He was *the* enemy. Mary had been right, of course. There could be naught between them, and this curiosity of hers, this draw to him that made Avelina wish to speak to him? 'Twas useless. Indeed, dangerous, if the look her brother gave her now was any indication.

When Niall sped up and rejoined his brother, Avelina said nothing. 'Twas for the best the two of them avoided each other. There was naught to say that wasn't tinged with hate and sadness and grief.

But just then, they stopped as riders approached. And what her enemy did next was something Avelina could not easily forget.

CHAPTER
SEVEN

Niall didn't even realize what he'd done until MacKinlay pulled his horse next to him. He'd seen the Clan MacBrannigan men and rode to her, positioning himself between Lady Avelina—Lina—and the warriors.

By now, all four of them, including his brother, had moved in front of her, but he'd made it too obvious at the start. Earning a glare from MacKinlay, one he deserved, Niall said nothing as the enemy clan approached.

Words were not needed.

Clan MacBrannigan neighbored Clan Mackenzie to the north, and though the two could not be considered allies, neither had they met in open battle. Unlike his clan and MacKinlay's, MacBrannigan's chief was unapologetically ruthless, though the fact still did not account for Niall's instinct to shield a woman who was also his enemy.

"You hide the lady as if we mean harm," one of the men —there were four—said as they approached. Though Niall and the others had ventured off the old Roman road into the grassy field beside it, they were still too close for his comfort.

"Be on your way," he said, not caring that MacKinlay continued to show his annoyance.

"We mean to do so," said the man in the lead. "But I find it curious to see you"—he nodded to MacKinlay—"riding beside the men who slaughtered your clan."

"I am the chief of Clan MacKinlay and will thank you not to speak of my ancestors."

The first man whistled. "Chief, aye?"

Niall was finished with this discussion. "Move along, or we will ensure it."

He said it low enough that it took a moment for the words to penetrate. When they did, MacBrannigan did not take kindly to the threat. However, Niall did not take kindly to their presence.

"My brother will not hesitate to engage you," Kieran said. "Mind that as you consider your next move."

The men looked back and forth between all four of them. Thus far, Fergus had remained silent, which was surprising given he'd been anything but in the hall.

"We seek no quarrel," the smallest of the four, riding in the back, said. "Move on," he added, and surprisingly, the others listened. He'd not been the one Niall would have expected to command the others' movements, but sometimes, 'twas not the loudest voice or biggest man, but the smartest among them who commanded respect. Clearly, they respected their clansman, because even though they had been one breath away from reaching for their swords, all four of them abandoned the thought and rode away.

"They are a long way from home," Fergus said when the men were no longer in hearing distance. So, the man did have a voice. Then he said to Niall, his tone accusatory, "You provoked them."

"Better to provoke them than say nothing."

"I can protect my sister."

That, from McKinlay.

"I can protect myself," she responded. Niall angled himself to see her. Indeed, he'd spotted the bow at her side and assumed she carried it for a reason. So, the woman was proficient with a bow. The fact did not surprise him.

"There is a river there." Kieran broke the tension, which had risen high after the altercation, by pointing northwest. "Perhaps we should water the horses and take a wee reprieve."

Niall would prefer to keep riding—the sooner they got to Glencloy, the sooner he could be away from his companions. Although, there was one companion, if he were being honest, Niall was not so ready to part from.

Without answering, he followed his brother toward the river. Eventually, he heard the sound of the horses behind him. The others silently joined them, though slightly upstream, as the riding party watered and fed their mounts. By the time Niall returned from relieving himself and opened the saddlebag, pulling out a dried piece of meat, Lina was gone. When she did appear through the thicket once again, Niall did not hesitate.

Her clansmen otherwise occupied near the riverbank, Lina, eating what appeared to be a slice of bread, stood near her mount. As he approached, she lifted it. "Baked this morn," she said. "Packed dutifully by my maid, who considers things I would not."

"Such as food for the journey?"

"Aye. Why did you move in front of me on the road?"

Though not prepared for the question, he should have

been. Lina MacKinlay was no modest maid. "I do not know."

Her head cocked to the side. "We are enemies," she said as if Niall were not aware.

"Aye," he agreed.

"Why, then, does my blood not boil as it should when you are near?"

Her boldness fascinated him. Niall had met no other like her. "Perhaps because you are so enthralled by me," he said, matching her boldness with his own, "that you forget to hate when I am near."

She seemed to consider his words.

"'Tis perhaps the same reason I moved to protect you when nothing should have been further from my mind, for many reasons."

"Such as?"

Her brother watched them.

"You are my enemy."

"That is all?"

"And you've clansmen to protect you."

"You forget, Niall, that I can protect myself. I do not bring my bow for decoration."

He took two steps toward her despite the glares of both her kinsmen. "Yet, your bow was not at the ready."

Her lips were fuller than any he'd ever seen before. What would they feel like gliding over his own? How sweet would the taste of Lina's tongue be? He would dearly like to find out, despite the fact he could not. Would not.

"I did not deem it necessary."

He smiled. "So you have seen many skirmishes, then, to know when 'tis necessary?"

"I've traveled with my brother, aye."

"And have you used your bow to injure or kill a man?"

"No, but I have used it to defend myself. And would not hesitate to drive an arrow into the neck of any man who threatened me or my kin and clan."

He did not doubt her words. "Why are you proficient with the bow, Lina?"

Her chin rose. She would not tell him, though Niall could guess at the reason. If his father and half his clan were slaughtered, he'd wish to do the same even if 'twas unusual to do so. He'd seen women wield a bow and arrow or even a sword but rarely. "Why did you come over here to speak to me?"

"Why do you not send me away?"

The answer to both was so obvious yet unbelievable at the same time. Niall was attracted to the sister of his clan's greatest enemy's chief. Attracted in a way that was both unrealistic and dangerous. But in matters of the heart, such things often mattered little.

"I would do so if I were able. But it seems my lips refuse to form the command."

Oh, this woman...

"Why do you smile so?" she asked. "As if you are reluctant to do so? Is smiling not encouraged in your clan?"

"I do so less than most," he admitted.

"Why?"

He felt the surprising desire to be honest or, at least, as best he could. "I've learned that emotion is unreliable."

She made a very unladylike, adorable sound. "I've not heard something as ridiculous as that before in my life."

"You have your opinion, and I have mine."

"What happened to make you believe as much?" Then, before he could answer, she added, "So you do not trust emotion?"

"I do not."

"Do you have them?"

"When I'm unable to stop myself."

Lina shook her head. "You are a most curious man, Niall Duncraig."

"You are a most curious woman, Avelina MacKinlay."

Their gazes locked. Neither of them turned or even, it seemed, breathed. He could see the rise and fall of her chest but tried not to notice that particular area too closely. Though it was difficult, out of the corner of his eye, not to do so.

"We had best be off."

Niall's brother approached, clearly worried about the fact that Lina's kinsmen stalked toward them looking as if they might have something to say about his extended conversation with the woman. Indeed, a most curious conversation. He'd expected them to discuss the MacBrannigan men or the weather, not the reason for his disdain for emotion. Or to admit, which they had basically both done, that they wished to be in each other's presence despite that they should both want just the opposite.

"Niall?"

Just before her brother arrived, he allowed himself to be pulled away.

"Aye," he said, following Kieran. But a backward glance confirmed what Niall had suspected. Lina still watched him with a curiosity and appreciation she did not bother to hide.

"You play a very dangerous game," his brother said, noticing the direction of his attention.

"I do," Niall admitted. "One I should end this very moment."

"You should," his brother agreed. Then, with a very loud, very long sigh, Kieran added, "But you will not."

CHAPTER
EIGHT

The very moment they stepped into the keep of Caerlaverock Castle, Ewan pulled Avelina aside.

"You will cease speaking with him, Lina."

Her brother had attempted to gain her attention during the remainder of their journey, but she and Niall had ridden together. She'd expected this conversation much sooner, but now would do.

"I will speak to whomever I please," she said, having rehearsed the line earlier. As Niall and his brother spoke to the steward, she continued in a hushed tone, "Including the laird of Duncraig."

"He is the son of the man who killed our father, Lina. And many others."

Her jaw dropped. "He is?" She pointed to Niall, whose back was to her. The hall, which was on the entrance level of the keep, lay before them. It appeared the evening meal was finished, but the steward escorted both Niall and his brother inside. For his part, Fergus waited for Ewan and Avelina near the entrance to the mostly empty hall. "That man, you say?"

Her brother was not amused. "Lina," he warned. But she would not give him further opportunity to tell her what she knew already. If there was one man in the world she should not wish to speak with, to have her heart race at the sight of him, to imagine kissing. . . 'twas the one who looked back even now as his eyes sought hers.

Though they'd spoken of little of consequence as they rode—only facts about each of them that most in their lives likely knew already—Avelina had begun to feel a softening toward Niall. That is, if she'd ever been truly hardened against the man.

"Ewan," she said back to him in the same tone. Though they were nearly the same age, the fact that her brother was chief of their clan lent him, at times, more of an authoritarian role over her. Which, she supposed, was real and not simply her own conjuring. If Ewan wished, he could have her married. She was, in fact, under his control. But rarely did he wield that control as chief and not simply as her brother, like he had attempted to do just now. "I am a grown woman. You know as much and know also how futile your efforts to command me will be."

His expression hardened. "If I wished it—"

"If you wished it, you could do so. Aye. But you have been there, by my side, for the death of our father. And our mother. And know your strength is my own. Your conviction, my own. And I do believe you trust I am able to make decisions as well as thee."

She knew it because Ewan had told her, more than once, that he was proud of the woman she was becoming. "Let us go into the hall before our host takes our absence as a slight against him. Though I will admit, I do not see him."

Avelina had met Laird Caerlaverock on more than once occasion, and he did not seem to be present at the moment.

A widower, he'd not yet remarried that Avelina was aware, and only four other Caerlaverock clansmen and two servants seemed to linger in the hall.

Her brother made a sound deep in his throat before relenting. The steward greeted them at the entrance to the hall, and while he and Ewan and Fergus spoke, Avelina looked toward the trestle table where Niall and his brother were seated.

He watched her every move.

Of course, her brother declined to sit with them, though the steward did not seem to think it odd. Likely he'd been more surprised to see them arrive together than he was to watch as Avelina, Ewan, and Fergus sat at the very opposite end of the hall. Immediately, servants came to them offering wine or ale and trenchers.

She sat across from Ewan with a perfect view of Niall. A fact he seemed to notice, the corners of his lips tugging upward as Avelina took her seat. Was he aware she sat this way, rather than offering him her back as Ewan did, apurpose?

It seemed, aye, he did.

"If you will look over there throughout the meal, perhaps you should sit next to me," Ewan said.

"You cannae continue to stare at the lad," Fergus, who sat beside Ewan, agreed.

Though Fergus was, indeed, older than Niall, he was not so much older as to warrant calling the chief's son a "lad."

"Nay?"

"Nay," he said, turning to Ewan for support.

"I told her as much," her brother said.

While the two men talked about how she should best behave, Avelina stole another glance Niall's way. He watched her as if he wished to laugh but didn't. Unbidden, a smile formed, a joy she could not place coursing through her.

He seemed to be the kind of man who did not smile often, and the sight of him now nearly doing so made Avelina break into a smile of her own.

"Lina!"

She sighed, not wishing to hear her brother scold her throughout the meal. As such, she tried, and often failed, not to look over Ewan's shoulder as she ate. Instead, she thought of the day when the spectators had returned from the king's horrific decree. At the time, 'twas simply called "the battle," but later it became known as the Battle of The Black Friars. She'd always found it curious that the battle had been held at a monastery, witnessed by the friars, who the king apparently held a strong affinity for but, in her opinion, should have stopped the bloodshed.

Perhaps remembering how much she'd lost that day would remind Avelina why her brother was wroth with her now. And 'twas not that day alone. She, and her brother, too, always believed that her mother's illness may not have led to her death had she not been also harboring a broken heart.

When she looked up again, Niall's attention was on his brother.

He'd not participated in the battle, but his father and clansmen had. And they'd taken everything from her and her family. Their clan had barely survived. Ewan, on this one occasion, was right. She should not be smiling at the laird of Duncraig.

"If we find the cattle where he claims," Fergus was saying, "what do you intend?"

She was curious about Ewan's answer too.

"They did not get there on their own. 'Tis too far a distance. Which means someone led them there. Who, and for what purpose? We will need to determine that in order to avoid a renewed war between our clans."

"I cannae think of who might wish to instigate such a war," Fergus said.

Avelina listened but did not participate in the men's discussion. The longer she thought about her behavior that day, the angrier she became at herself. When the meal was finished, they stood and were escorted from the hall by the steward. Avelina did not look back once, but as she and her brother were separated, Avelina taken to a different section of the keep, she was surprised to hear the very voice she'd been chastising herself for speaking with.

"Pardon," Niall said to the maid behind her. "Are you taking her to the Thistle Chamber?"

"Indeed, my lord," the maid said as all three of them paused in the otherwise empty corridor.

"If you would open it, I know the way and will escort her there in a moment."

The maid looked between them, but before Avelina could inform her there was no need, she bobbed a quick curtsy. Niall's commanding presence left little room for anything but obedience, and she hurried away.

"Why do you look at me so differently this eve?" he asked the moment the maid turned the corner.

The corridor was small, Niall standing close enough that if Avelina reached out, she could touch him. Light from the wall torch made his expression easy enough to discern. Concern was etched on his face.

"My brother and Fergus reminded me that you are not a man I should have become so familiar with so quickly. Or at all."

"And you allow others' opinions to sway your own so easily?"

"I allow myself to be reminded of what I lost at your clan's hands."

"My clan, aye. I cannae deny it. But I was neither in that battle nor would I have wished such an ill to befall you, Lina."

The words were more softly spoken than she'd heard from him since they met.

"You are a hard man," she blurted, "are you not?"

His lips pressed together. "I can be, aye."

"Yet you tread gently with me. Why do you care, Laird Niall of Duncraig, if I should stop gazing your way during the meal? Or remind myself that you are my enemy?"

His eyes bored into her own. "If you must remind yourself we are enemies," he said, "perhaps. . . we are not."

"You are the Duncraig's son. I am the daughter of the man he slayed. Of course, we are enemies."

"I am naught but a man, and you, a woman, both of us but children during the Battle of The Black Friars."

Aye, he was a man indeed.

"And still, you do not answer me. Why does it matter to you? In a few days, we will never see each other again."

He did not answer. Instead, Niall continued to stare at her, but Avelina did not look away. She did attempt to slow the beating of her heart at his continued gaze but otherwise said nothing. Moved not at all.

"It should not," he said finally, as if admitting something he did not wish to.

"Indeed." Avelina would have told him he was right, and it should not matter. They should not be speaking now and should probably not speak again at length for the remainder of the trip. And yet, she said none of that. Instead, she watched as he took a step toward her.

She stared mutely as he reached up and clasped a strand of errant hair between his fingers. Tucking it behind her ear, his hand remained there for a bit longer than necessary, as if 'twas unnecessary to fix her hair at all.

Avelina did not move. She wasn't even sure she continued to breathe.

Of course, you are breathing, you silly girl.

"This," she said, her voice hardly sounding like her own, "is highly inappropriate. Speaking to each other alone. That, even more so," she said as his hand finally, and sadly, returned to his side.

"I will leave you then," he said, but Niall did not make a move to do so.

"Wait."

He did. The reason she called him back had not needed to be voiced. 'Twas wrong. And aye, highly inappropriate. Yet, 'twas unmistakable too. That Avelina did not want him to leave was as infuriating as the fact that she'd wished for that very thing not long ago.

"Will you speak with me on the morrow? Or do we begin the day as enemies once again?" He asked her to decide. Was Niall simply a Duncraig, one of the most important members of that clan, and the bitterest of MacKinlay enemies? Or was he simply a man whose name held more ill will than she wished?

Fact was, the answer was both.

Would she speak with him on the morrow? Avelina was unsure if she could avoid doing so. Unsure if she wished to avoid it.

Instead of saying any of that, however, she simply said, "I will speak with you."

For him, that seemed to be enough. "Come. I will show you to your chamber."

She followed, asking what she'd been curious about earlier. "You've stayed here before to know this keep so well."

"Aye," he said. "Many times. Caerlaverock is an ally to Clan Duncraig."

"And to Clan MacKinlay as well."

Niall stopped and turned. "It seems, then, we've at least one thing in common."

As they looked into each other's eyes, Avelina observed, "I think it is not the only thing."

"Aye," Niall agreed. "I fear you might be right."

Avelina shared that fear. And with it, the knowledge that it may be too late to turn back from whatever they'd started.

CHAPTER NINE

Niall had avoided her all morn. Not because he'd wanted to, but because her brother had and his man had been glaring at him since they broke their fast, and Niall had no wish to altercate with either of them. Convincing the pair they must investigate the errant cattle to avoid a war with his father would be difficult enough without this added complication.

There was no doubt, Avelina was a complication.

He should not have gone to her last eve. But her change in demeanor had bothered him enough that he had not been able to resist despite his brother's admonitions. Both last eve and now.

"You court trouble, Niall," Kieran said as they slowed their mounts. Having ridden since sunrise, it was time for a brief respite for the horses. And for Avelina. Surely she was not accustomed to riding for so many hours?

"Indeed," he agreed.

"Why do it?" Kieran asked, correctly surmising that Niall was about to seek her out now that Lina was separated from her men. She sat on a rock by the riverbank, peering into its depths. He understood the draw as Niall, too, loved the water. Castle MacKinlay had the advantage of being directly positioned on the sea, so Lina must crave it more than most.

"I cannae answer that completely," Niall said as he approached her, leaving Kieran to his sounds of exasperation.

Avelina wore a different gown than she had the day before, this one a deep blue that complimented her well—though he suspected any color would do as much. Niall was surprised by the rapid beating of his heart as she turned. This was no battle he was about to enter that he should feel such... unease.

Or perhaps it was. One without swords and bloodshed, with the wounds they would create deep inside hurting nearly as much. He'd been in love once and did not recommend the state. His wife, when he found a woman suitable for the role, would care for him, aye. As he would her. But love? Nay.

"Have you changed your mind?" he asked, approaching. "Or will you still speak with me today?"

She turned.

Dammit, the woman was beautiful. A MacKinlay. The MacKinlay's sister. Of all the women he should wish to speak with, she was not the one he'd have chosen.

"'Tis you who have avoided me," she said, her assessment correct.

"The daggers in your brother's eyes prevented me from seeking you out sooner."

She glanced in her brother's direction, though he seemed to be remaining in place near the horses. At least, for now.

"You do not strike me as a man to let such a thing deter him," she said as he sat on the other end of her rock.

"I am not," he admitted. "But if your brother is deterred for any reason from learning why his cattle graze on our land, I fear naught I can say will prevent the beginnings of a renewed feud."

"I fear this"—she waved her hand between them—"could do such a thing."

"Aye," Niall agreed, "it could."

"So it was likely a good enough idea that you should avoid me, and I, in turn, should do the same."

"It was."

"And yet, here we are."

"Indeed."

Niall had never been a man to be anything but direct. "I enjoy speaking with you, Lina," he said. "'Tis why I am here."

"I enjoy speaking with you," she said immediately, leaving no doubt that her words were true. "Though I should not."

"A fact we've well established."

"Look," she exclaimed as a fish leaped from the water and dove back into the river. "I've not seen such a thing in all my life."

"Nay? Keep watching and 'tis likely you will see it again. They are quite common here."

She did but nothing emerged. If Niall could have reached into the water and forced the fish to leap above it simply to see that expression of wonder again, he'd have done it.

"You are a beautiful woman, Lina." The words spilled from his lips without warning. "Though I'm certain you've been told so many, many times."

"None by a man who. . ." She stopped abruptly. Lina looked down to her lap, where her hands were suddenly clasped. 'Twas a gesture from her that Niall did not expect. Her boldness seemed to have entirely disappeared.

"Who?" he prompted. Though perhaps 'twas not gentlemanly to do so, he wanted to know her response.

When Lina glanced back to her brother, who had still not moved to remove Niall from her presence, he knew the direction of her thoughts, ones he had previously only suspected.

"I cannae."

"Aye, lass, you can."

Her eyes met his. Niall willed her to continue.

"'Tis not appropriate for me to say."

"Good."

She startled. "Pardon me?"

He repeated himself. "Good. I look forward to it even more now. A man who..."

Her chin rose. A flash of the woman who insisted to her brother she would be making this journey was all he needed to pull her out even further. So, it seemed the woman was bold, except for this one topic. Because she had little experience with men? Seemed likely given her station.

"Say it, Lina." He did not ask but demanded.

"Not by a man who made my stomach twist and turn and not in a bad way. Rather a pleasant one, as if there were butterflies in there that came down from my chest to invade every part of me. 'Tis the oddest feeling and not one to which I'm accustomed. And that, Niall, is what I had been prepared to say when I stopped. Do you now see why I've done so?"

"Because you had your first rousing of true desire,

directed toward me? I see only what I wish to see, Lina. And that is the admission you just gave me."

"What will you do with it?"

Though Niall could not believe a woman as beautiful as she had not been courted by many men, that she'd desired none of them was the even more surprising revelation. Nearly as much as the admission. . . she desired him.

The feeling was mutual.

"What do you wish I could do with the knowledge?"

Her eyes went to his lips. Ahh, so a kiss, then. That was easily done and innocent enough.

"I. . ." She seemed reluctant to admit it.

He did not wish to see her tortured. "If I had the opportunity, there is naught I'd wish for more than to kiss you, Lina. Of course, 'twould be highly inappropriate, especially given our status—"

"As enemies."

"Aye, as enemies." He smiled. "Or at least, the clan's status as enemies. And yet. . ." He looked at her lips, full and extremely kissable. "I will do so despite the impropriety of it."

When she realized the full import of his words, Lina's eyes widened. She swallowed, and by all that was holy, Lina's tongue actually peeked out as she ever so briefly licked her top lip. Probably not even realizing she'd done it, Lina let her gaze drop to Niall's lips. There was no question what she was thinking now.

Incredibly, at the mere thought of her lips on his, Niall found himself needing to shift his position. A kiss. What an innocent thing. And yet, something about the idea of kissing her. . .

'Tis because she is forbidden. The sister of your greatest enemy.

Perhaps. Or perhaps there was something more. Certainly, there was more to Lina than simply being the MacKinlay chief's sister. Even now, her eyes blazed with defiance, though he was uncertain who she defied.

"Avelina," an annoyed voice called.

He should have noticed her brother approaching, but Niall had been too intent on staring at Lina's lips.

Her sigh of annoyance made him smile. But for this, he would not allow her to suffer. Jumping from the rock, Niall approached his enemy.

"She sat here alone when I joined her. If you will be displeased with someone, be so with me, MacKinlay."

"You've not to ask me such a thing when you know I'm displeased with you, and your clan, already. But talking with my sister—"

"Is it a worse offense than being the son of the man who killed your father?"

As expected, MacKinlay rushed to Niall. His fist would have connected with Niall's cheek had he not stepped away quickly enough. MacKinlay did manage to grab his waist, however, but it was Avelina's voice Niall heard as the two men were knocked to the ground.

She dinnae call to her brother but to Niall. Her voice penetrated at the same time as his brother's and another man's, Fergus, obviously. He allowed himself to be easily pulled from MacKinlay, who was somewhat more reluctant to quit the fight.

Niall would dearly love to land one square punch to the man's face, but doing so would not endear himself to Lina. And, like it or nay, he wanted to endear himself to her. For that reason, he allowed himself to be led away by his brother. Or began to, at least, until he heard him tell Lina that the matter "dinnae concern" her.

"How could it not concern her?" he asked as his brother attempted to pull him back. "If Avelina hadn't spoken with me—"

"Keep my sister's name from your filthy mouth, whoreson," MacKinlay spat.

"Perhaps ask your sister if I should keep her name from my mouth. Or do her thoughts on the matter mean so little to you?"

"That's enough, Niall," Kieran tried to warn him.

"You dare lecture my chief about his sister?" Fergus was as angry as Niall had ever seen him, including when they were near-attacked on the road.

"I lecture no one," Niall said. "I simply—"

"Shall we not be on the road?" Lina cut in. "To get to the cattle by sundown? Or do we relish finding shelter together again for the evening?"

Such a prospect was not one he relished at all. Her brother mumbled something as he and Fergus seemed to agree, for now, not to attack Niall. Once again, Avelina was the one to see them through the disagreement.

"Aye," Kieran said. "We shall."

Reluctantly agreeing with Lina, Niall turned away one final time and stalked toward the horses. He did not look back until well and truly mounted, with he and his brother riding ahead of the others.

So rarely riled the way he just had been, Niall was further convinced there was something special about Lina. His only regret over the incident?

He'd not been able to kiss her.

CHAPTER
TEN

"Nay, I will not discuss it further."

Avelina and her brother had been arguing since he attacked Niall. And aye, she agreed Niall may have deserved it for provoking Ewan, but if her brother had not approached them as if she'd done something wrong, perhaps Niall would not have found it necessary to come to her defense.

And he had done so, the thought of which Avelina could not get from her head. As they passed the verdant green mountains—unfamiliar territory she had never thought to ride on as they'd crossed the border onto Duncraig land earlier—she watched him ride. Waiting for those times, he turned back to look at her. They were few, but when he did, Avelina's heart leapt. As it did when she thought of what he'd said.

If I had the opportunity, there is naught I'd wish for more than to kiss you, Lina.

She'd thought of nothing else. Well, perhaps except her brother's reaction. Her clan's reaction to what they would see as a betrayal. Except, Avelina had begun to think beyond a kiss. To the ramifications of falling for the son of the man who'd killed her father in battle. Yet, Niall had not said he wished to marry her, for goodness sakes. Nor would she ever consider such a thing.

'Twas but a simple kiss. If there was a way for it to happen, would she do it?

Aye, she would.

"There." Niall turned his mount back toward them. His attention was on the dots that Avelina could see now in the distance. Her brother and Fergus sat up straighter in their saddles, as did she. "Come," her brother said, spurring his mount forward.

Their two riding parties sped toward the hill where, as they approached, the cattle were easy enough to see. As Niall had said, there were more than twenty, though Avelina could not discern to whom they belonged. Sure enough, however, as the others dismounted, with the cattle quite alone grazing in the fields before them, it did not take long for confirmation.

Her brother inspected just two of the cattle before turning to Fergus and speaking rapidly to him. Avelina couldn't hear what they spoke of from this distance, but she could imagine.

She'd been about to dismount when Niall appeared out of nowhere below her. Though she did not need his assistance, Avelina accepted it for the simple fact that she wished to touch his hand. Whether he aided her for that reason, or simply to be courteous, she neither knew nor cared.

The touch was precisely as she imagined it would be. His hand, as firm as anyone's. But it was the way he looked at her that made the moment so much more than simply a gallant knight assisting a lady from her mount.

"My brother will not be pleased," she said as her feet touched the ground. "Added to the fact that the cattle are clearly ours."

Unfortunately, he dropped her hand as they walked slowly toward the others. Ewan and Fergus were arguing. Niall's brother stood off to the side, his arms crossed, his lips tugged upward in the slightest of smiles.

"I dinnae think Fergus believed you."

"Nay," Niall said, her brother and Fergus's conversation now clear. "He did not."

"Never on their own," Ewan was saying now. "Who or why?"

It was the question she'd been pondering as well. Who would have led cattle to this spot? To Avelina, the answer as to "why" was an obvious one.

Suddenly everyone seemed to be talking at once. Discussing how the cattle got to this spot. Where they would have come from and who may have aided them. They also discussed how to get them back.

In the end, it was decided she and Fergus would return home, where a party would be fetched to retrieve the cattle, and Ewan would travel to the chief of Clan Tannochbrae, over whose land the cattle must have been led to arrive here. Fergus was reluctant to leave his chief's side but, remarkably, since Niall and his brother insisted on joining Ewan, he finally agreed.

"I am coming with you," Avelina declared to Ewan as they began to set out already, even having just arrived. Fergus would be forced to sleep under the stars, but if they left immediately, Ewan believed they could reach Tannochbrae Manor by nightfall.

"Nay, you are not."

It seemed she had been arguing with her brother since

Niall arrived at their home. But there was no help for it. She simply refused to be separated from Niall yet.

"I am," she said, returning to her horse and mounting as the others did. When she rode up to her brother, Avelina stuck out her chin and dared her brother to defy her. She tried to conjure a time when she'd wanted something within her power to achieve and failed. Avelina could not think of such a time. Her brother knew it well.

And she wanted to be with Niall Duncraig.

'Twas absurd. Illogical. Not at all characteristic of her, since losing herself over a man was not Avelina's style. And yet, despite her strength and resolve, something about him had crept into her soul. A quality she could not name but had quickly made him the focus of her thoughts. Denying it was as futile as pretending to her brother there was any reason she wished to accompany him to Tannochbrae Manor but the opportunity to be with Niall.

For the first time since her brother attempted to waylay her, she looked at Niall. 'Twas rare to see him smiling, and he did just that. As if her defiance of her brother pleased him, and why shouldn't it? Ewan was Niall's greatest enemy and the reason she should not wish to be with him. The reason she should cease thinking of kissing him. But as their eyes locked, Avelina knew with certainty she'd do neither of those things.

In fact, the opposite was true.

Then they began to move. The next phase of their journey, begun.

CHAPTER
ELEVEN

By the time they reached Tannochbrae Manor, their riding party had grown quiet. It had been a long day, and yet, Lina had not once asked to stop more than they had for very brief respites for their mounts. She rode as well as any of them, and Niall could not help but be impressed by her.

The chieftain of Clan Tannochbrae was an old man who had managed to remain allies with both Duncraig and MacKinlay. As they were escorted into the hall, though the chieftain had clearly been abed already, wall torches lighting their way, he greeted them personally.

"If King Alexander had been at my door, I'd have been less surprised than to learn the Duncraig second and the MacKinlay chief had arrived here together."

Their small party was an odd one, indeed, and since they'd come into the gates they had caused a stir, even at this late hour. There were at least ten or so retainers now gathered, listening.

"Many thanks for receiving us at this late hour," he began. "You know my brother Kieran," Niall said.

"Aye, and good den to you," the chieftain said.

"And to you." Kieran inclined his head.

"And how, pray tell, do you find yourself among them?" Tannochbrae asked.

"A tale best told privately," MacKinlay said. "You've met my sister, Lady Avelina, aye?"

Lina approached the old man, a widower of many years. His age did not diminish his ability to appreciate her beauty. Taking her hand and kissing it at Lina's slight bow, the chieftain smiled kindly at her. Niall understood easily the man's rapture with her. Lina brought those around her into a spell that was not at all cunning. It simply. . .was.

"Are you hungry, my lady?" he asked her.

"Indeed," she said.

The chieftain's hearty laugh at her honest answer was followed by directives to the steward. This time, however, they were not to be seated separately since one trestle table was hastily prepared for them. The chieftain himself sat with their odd group, ordering everyone, with the exception of the two maids who served them ale and stew, from the hall.

Niall attempted to ignore her, but Lina sat directly across from him, so there was no hope for that. Instead, he would simply endure her brother's glares and even Kieran's own annoyed ones. He and his brother rarely disagreed on matters of import, but Lina was clearly an exception.

He told the chieftain of their discovery, the journey to MacKinlay, and finding the cattle just as he and his brother had left them. It did not take long for Tannochbrae to understand why they visited his hall.

"I will make inquiries on the morrow," he said. "That many cattle do not find their way across my land without notice. And 'tis certain they came this way."

"Aye," MacKinlay agreed. "If any of your people saw their movement... or who could have led them there..."

"Do you have suspects?" he asked.

Niall and MacKinlay's eyes met. The chief was revealing little, but surely he must have someone in mind.

"'Tis too soon to discern," the chief said finally. "But 'tis someone who wishes for our feud to begin anew."

"You can think of none," Kieran asked, "who would wish such a thing?"

As usual, the MacKinlay chief appeared less than pleased to be forced to converse with them. He would be cordial to his brother, though. Niall would ensure it.

"I can think of none who would be pleased to sit at this table as I do—"

"Ewan," Lina admonished.

Their host chuckled.

"But neither does one person come to my mind as an obvious suspect. Our clan has grown these past years, and I cannae pretend to know the motives of all its people."

Round and round they went until, finally, the meal was consumed. Enough ale to fill Niall for two evenings had been drunk, and Lina appeared as tired as he'd expect her to be.

"Perhaps we should reconvene on the morrow."

Niall must have been looking at Lina, because her brother did the same. Her eyes widened, as if proving she was indeed awake and aware, but 'twas too late. When the MacKinlay chief then gave Niall a look as if to say, *She is not yours to concern yourself about*, Niall ignored him.

"Come." Their host stood. "I will have you shown to your chambers, which are already prepared for you. On the morrow, I will make inquiries. In the meantime, you are my guests. If 'tis possible for your clans to make peace in this keep, then I shall gladly be the host to such an occasion."

The look MacKinlay gave Niall refuted their host's words. Neither was Niall inclined to make peace with the man, even if his feelings for the sister had become something of a problem. Thoughts of her occupied him when she was not in his direct line of vision. And when she was? Little was left for him to imagine as the woman made even the slightest movement. A lick of the lips. A peek at him, something she did often, though not as often as he'd like. When she shifted on her mount or adjusted her gown, Niall noticed all of it.

His promise of kissing her was never far from his mind.

"This way, my lady," a maid said, guiding Lina away. By luck or fate, she did so directly his way. On a whim, as she passed him, Niall took advantage of the others' distraction and whispered, "Leave it open a crack."

Her head whipped toward him as Lina continued to be led away. Her eyes were wide, questioning. But Niall could say no more. Did she understand? Would she do it?

He would find out soon enough.

CHAPTER
TWELVE

Surely he had not meant...

Avelina paced the comfortable chamber. Though a manor house, Tannochbrae was nearly as large as her own keep, and the size of bedchambers reflected as much. The maid had prepared warm water for her to wash with, and now in nothing more than her shift, having used the lavender soap to scrub every bit of skin she could, Avelina could not lie in the bed. Surely he would not risk coming to her chamber. As the hour grew even later, she began to doubt she had heard the words correctly. Still, something kept her awake, the remnants of sleepiness she'd felt at the supper table long gone.

Back and forth she walked, sometimes over to the hearth, staring at the fire so long her eyes began to burn. And then back toward the canopied bed, where she resumed her pacing.

Just as she began to contemplate crawling into the very inviting-looking bed, its cream coverlet seeming to call her name, a quick knock at the door was followed by its opening.

Niall.

His shoulders filled the frame and then he moved inside quickly, the wooden door clicking shut behind him.

It was as if she had to relearn how to breathe. Niall's presence in her bedchamber was so much more intimidating than in the hall or the open fields. His promise of a kiss was never far from her mind, but it was certainly not so now as he closed the distance between them.

"I was not certain you heard me," he said, stopping short of her. His eyes dipped, and Avelina was never more aware of her own body than she was at this moment.

"I was not certain I had either," she admitted.

Why did he appear so much larger in this chamber?

"I'd have come sooner, but I wanted to be sure I was not followed."

"By my brother?"

"Aye."

"Because you should not be in here."

He laughed. "Certainly not."

She simply had to know. "Are you here to kiss me?"

He breathed in deeply, watching her, as if undecided. Avelina would not leave this to chance. Taking a step toward him, wanting very much to feel his lips on hers, she was about to reach up when Niall made a sound halfway between a groan and a growl. He reached her in one stride. Niall cupped both of her cheeks, holding her head and forcing it upward. They were strong, capable hands, and yet held her so gently she could have cried. If not for the other type of feelings coursing through her.

Avelina's heart slammed in her chest as Niall's head lowered. At the first touch of his lips, Avelina closed her eyes. His lips were both hard and soft, somehow exactly how she imagined. But then his tongue was there—something she'd not experienced during any stolen kisses her suitors had taken. Running along the crease of her lips, 'twas as if he wanted her to open her mouth for him. And so, she did.

Suddenly, his head slanted as Niall's tongue was once again there, demanding from her that she touched her own tongue to his. And so, she did, and was rewarded for it by another groan. This time, she could feel the vibrations of the sound on her lips, and she made one of her own.

Now his tongue did not just touch hers but swirled around it. As Niall's lips moved over hers, his tongue became increasingly demanding, and Avelina was glad to give him what he silently demanded.

The kiss deepened.

She learned quickly, her arms now around his waist and Niall's hands still on her face, holding it in place as if she would dare leave. There was no place in the world Avelina would rather be at that moment but in this man's arms, learning how to kiss properly.

When he pulled away, she wanted to fight him. To beg him to continue. But he did so only enough to look at her, his eyes penetrating deep into her soul.

"That was your first."

"Like that? Aye. I've been kissed before, but never. . ."

"I understand," he said, ensuring she did not have to. "But know this, Lina. Kissing does not always feel this way."

He was so close she could smell the fresh soap he used to cleanse himself. Lina could feel his breath and wanted so very much to kiss him again.

"Does it not?"

He slowly shook his head. "Nay. It does not."

He leaned down once again, his hands moving from her

cheeks to around her shoulders. It was as if she were being consumed by him, engulfed in Niall's embrace. If the kiss was not enough, being held to his chest, Avelina felt his body against hers...

She gripped the material of his tunic as Niall's mouth opened even more widely. Her very core clenched. Avelina had never experienced such a feeling before. It startled her enough to pull away. Looking up into his eyes, she asked the silent question, already knowing the answer. Or suspecting, at least. Mary had told her a bit, enough for Avelina to consider this must be what her maid referenced.

"Your desire scares you?" Niall asked, his voice deep and low. Soothing too.

"I've never felt that before," she admitted, still engulfed in his arms.

"Tell me."

"It's just, when you kiss me. Hold me against you like this..."

"Go on."

She shook her head. "I cannae."

His jaw flexed, and Avelina resisted the urge to reach up and touch it to see if the angles were as hard as they appeared. But she didn't dare pull her arms away from him.

"Between your legs," he said, vocalizing what she could not. "Aye?"

"Aye."

"Desire, Lina. I feel it too."

"'Tis a powerful feeling."

He chuckled. "Men have died for it."

"I think perhaps I would too."

In response to that, he lowered his head once again. This time, he offered no quarter. Niall's tongue tangled with hers, the rhythm of their kiss so natural it was a wonder this was her first time. That the two of them had not been kissing each other forever.

It was there again. Avelina didn't even realize she was pressing against him until she felt him against her. Their hips circled each other's, and that's when she knew. This was a precursor to what it would be like to make love to a man such as Niall.

"Mmmm, Lina," he said, pulling away. This time, he took a full step back. The expression on his face underscored the fact that he moved away from her. "A kiss is just a kiss. But we dance around more that cannae be explored between us. I should have known. Should have realized this was not a good idea."

"I think 'tis a good idea indeed. That felt. . ." She sighed. "Like something I would like to do again."

He made a sound low in his throat. "As would I. Very much. But I fear it was too good—"

"How can a kiss be too good?" she genuinely wondered. "It seems such a thing is not possible."

"And yet." He licked his lips, Avelina spying that tongue which had so recently been inside her mouth. How she would like it to be again. . . "This was a mistake."

She disagreed. "You do not truly believe that?"

"I do."

"Why?" To her, 'twas just the opposite. Her heart sank that he felt otherwise.

"Because I'm experienced enough to realize, or should have realized, there was more between us."

"More? More than what?"

"More than just the desire for a simple kiss."

Neither said anything for some time.

"I should go," Niall began.

Lina reached out her hand, stopping him. His shoulder

was muscled, strong, beneath her fingertips. "I do not wish for you to leave."

"Neither do I wish it, but 'tis wise. You are not mine to take, Lina. And there's naught more I wish to do at this moment than to make you mine. To pull you into my arms, kiss you again, undress you, love you."

Shivers ran from her neck downward at his words. She wished for the same. But, of course, he was right. That could not be.

Unless. . .

"There is one way."

Again, they looked at one another, neither breaking eye contact.

"Lina. . ."

He seemed to know precisely what Avelina was thinking. The question was, had she really said as much aloud? Had she actually meant it? For they both knew that the only way was for them to become husband and wife. And surely she did not wish to take the eldest son of the Duncraig clan chief to husband.

Did she?

She dropped her hand. "I know not what I am saying. Of course, 'tis a silly notion." She laughed uncomfortably. "One taste of desire, and I speak of such things as. . ."

Though Avelina's hand dropped to her side, he captured it. Brought it to his lips.

"Marriage," he finished for her, kissing the top of her hand. "I've thought little on the matter." Niall turned her hand over, palm upward. "Though my parents wish otherwise."

He kissed the center of her palm and then her fingers. Then the tips of her fingers.

"Certainly, they would have something to say about me

taking a MacKinlay as a wife." He then kissed the tip of her pointer finger, just before he wrapped his lips around it.

Avelina swallowed.

He took her finger in deeper, suckled it. That feeling assaulted her once again, the one between her legs. "Niall. . ."

He stopped. Unfortunately. "Aye, 'tis a silly notion indeed."

Of course, he was right.

"And one we should discuss further." He dropped her hand.

Avelina's heart raced. Had he truly said. . .

"'Tis madness," she said.

"Aye."

"To even consider such a thing."

"Indeed."

"We are enemies."

"Our clans, are, aye." Niall smiled. "But it seems we've proven this eve that we are not."

She swallowed.

"If I do not leave your chamber, there will be no thought or discussion on the matter. We will, instead, make a rash decision." He smiled. "Though admittedly, 'twould be an enjoyable one."

It was as if her entire life had just shifted.

CHAPTER
THIRTEEN

N iall would not, could not, marry Lady Avelina MacKinlay.

"You are awake still?"

Kieran had been discovered, lost, after the Battle of The Black Friars. Despite Niall's parents' best efforts, none knew from where he came. He had not yet seen ten summers, but no clan or family had claimed him, and after a season had passed, it had been decreed he was now a part of their family. More than that, a son. A brother to Niall, his only sibling after his mother had nearly died giving birth to him, making it impossible for her to do so again. Niall rarely thought of Kieran as anything other than a full brother. But now, knowing what he was about to say. . . a rare seed of doubt as to Kieran's possible response to his intentions crept into his mind.

"Aye," Niall said. 'Twas unlikely he would sleep much this eve.

Though he was glad to have a private chamber, 'twas small. Much smaller than Lina's. His brother was in a second bed next to his, and Niall had been listening to his steady breathing, assuming Kieran had been sleeping. Perhaps he had.

"Did you just wake?" Kieran asked.

"Aye. You know 'tis difficult for me to remain asleep for long."

"You went to see her."

'Twas not a question, so Niall did not answer. Until his brother pressed him.

"I know not your intentions, Niall, but as I said before, 'tis a dangerous game you play."

Niall knew it well. "My intentions," he repeated, not having any more to offer.

"You cannae defile such a woman. Nor," he added quickly, before Niall could respond, "would I expect it of you."

The lone candle flickering between them did little to illuminate his brother's face, but as Niall turned onto his side and looked toward the man who knew him best in this world, he considered saying the words that swirled through his mind.

"Nay," he said, "I would not."

Kieran turned his head toward Niall. Though he could not see his eyes, Niall could imagine them. Where his might be judgmental, cold even, Kieran's would be warm. Kind. Curious.

"I am drawn to her," he said finally. "Drawn to her in a way I've not been drawn to any woman."

His brother sighed heavily, clearly not pleased to hear it.

Niall continued, "She is an enemy, aye. Or should be."

"But is not. At least to you?"

"Nay," he admitted. "She is not my enemy."

"But she is to our clan."

On that, his brother was accurate.

"I kissed her," he said. "And would have done more if I stayed in her chamber."

"The reason you should not have been in her chamber at all."

He'd not deny it. "She could not be more innocent. Yet her kiss awoke something in me."

The words sounded strange to his own ears, so Niall imagined they sounded the same to his brother. Indeed, Kieran did not respond for a time.

"I remember that night clearly."

A chill ran through him. Niall knew which night his brother referred to even if they rarely discussed it.

"But more than Father's shouts and your apologies, I remember most your expression. The idea that you'd been responsible for the healer's injury. . . you are a good man, Niall. 'Twas an accident—"

"Nay." He rejected the thought. "'Twas no accident that we jested with her."

"None believed the woman's story, nor do they now. That she is visited by the devil? That she plays cards with him?" Kieran made a sound.

"Neither did that mean we should have pretended to be that very devil. If she'd not chased us that night and fell. . ."

"She would not have twisted her ankle. Would not walk with a limp and now a cane. Aye, I know it well. And do not fully pardon what you did, but also wish to remind you that you are a good man despite a bad decision in your youth."

"A bad decision the healer pays the price for even now as an old woman."

"Do you not think 'tis time to forgive yourself? I reminisce on it only to tell you the man who refuses to allow himself to be spontaneous, who plots and plans and buries his emotions so deeply. . . that was not the man I always knew. And so if you kissed her, then I say, so be it. At least the younger version of my brother is not long dead."

"A good reminder of the consequences of being rash."

Kieran sighed heavily. "'Twas not the point I tried to make, Brother."

"But one you made well enough anyway. I shall not kiss her again."

"A decision I agree with."

"You confuse me, Brother. Advising caution and then carelessness and then caution again."

"I advise nothing but only share my thoughts. That you play a dangerous game with Lady Avelina, but that 'tis good to see you... alive as well."

"That does little to aid my decision."

"What decision is that?"

He could not say the words. Instead, Niall amended, "How to proceed. I do not wish to let her be, but neither do I wish to start the very war we are here to prevent."

"I cannae tell you how to proceed, only that I know no other man who I respect more than you, Brother. Whatever you decide, 'tis the right decision for you. Just understand, 'tis more than a woman with whom you trifle. The reason I remind you speaking with her, kissing her, 'tis dangerous indeed."

As if Niall needed the reminder.

Though grateful for Kieran's compliment, as he felt the same of his brother, he was no less confused now than before. Perhaps more so.

Trusting himself had led to a poor woman's injury, a harmless jest proving to be anything but harmless at all. But this was very different. He was no longer a young man but the second to the chief of his clan. A warrior. A man who made decisions only after long consideration.

Which was precisely what he needed to do now. Think about it. Consider more. Lina would continue to travel with them, which meant he had time. And in that time, perhaps an answer would come to him. Because as of this eve, the situation seemed an impossible one.

Leave the woman be. Do not talk to her. Touch her. Kiss her.

Certainly, do not make love to her.

A prospect that left him surprisingly empty.

The other alternative did not leave him empty but terrified. 'Twas madness. Recklessness. A thought he should not be having.

Marriage. To a MacKinlay. Nay, never.

'Twas his last thought as Niall closed his eyes and let sleep take him.

CHAPTER
FOURTEEN

Thankfully, her brother had gone hunting with their host after they'd broken their fast. Avelina had grown weary of his warnings and looks and judgments, as if she'd not already been judging herself since meeting Niall.

While the chieftain was having inquiries made, insisting they remain as guests in his keep in the meantime, he'd offered Avelina a maid, who had even brought a fresh gown that morn. Though the fit was not perfect, she was grateful for it, though she had no notion of its origins. The maid knew only that she'd been made to fetch it from the laundress.

Lifting the gown so she may walk easier, Avelina made her way to the garden behind the keep, which she'd been encouraged to explore. It seemed they would be here at least a day or two, and though she would dearly love to practice with her bow, Avelina was fully aware such an activity would be frowned upon.

She approached the most vivid violet fairy flowers Avelina had ever seen. Bending down, she took the petals in her hand, the color in stark contrast to her palm. Though she loved them dearly, Avelina had never been able to keep flowers alive well, the gardener jesting often about her inability to do so. But she adored them in her bedchamber, and as Avelina pulled the petal to her nose and breathed in deeply, she could almost forget the situation she found herself in currently.

Almost.

It was difficult to fully forget what she and Niall had discussed last eve. 'Twas even more difficult to forget his lips on hers. Avelina closed her eyes. She could almost feel them now, gliding across her own. His tongue, sweeping inside her mouth and claiming hers. Niall's body pressed against her.

Avelina's eyes flew open.

Somehow, she'd sensed him.

Standing near the garden's entrance, his arms crossed in front of him, the very man of whom she'd just been thinking stood there. Watching her.

Pulling her hand away and standing, Avelina otherwise did not move. Though they were alone now, anyone could come upon them, the garden a wide-open space.

"You are not hunting?"

"With your brother? Nay."

He made his way toward her, his presence looming with each step. For such a large man, larger than most, he moved quickly.

"A new gown?"

"Offered to me by our host."

"Beautiful, as always."

The compliment rolled off his tongue so easily she did not rebuke it as hollow as she did with most men's compliments of her. The sincerity of his words made Avelina's cheeks flush with a pleasure she could not deny.

"Thank you," she said simply, unable to cease looking at his lips. The simple truth was Avelina wanted him to kiss her again. To distract herself, Avelina said, "Tell me of yourself."

The request seemed to take him by surprise. Niall laughed, a rarer sound than Avelina would have liked.

"There is much to tell. What would you wish to know?"

"Hmm. I wish to know why you do not smile as often as your brother."

"I do not?"

"Nay, you do not."

It seemed as if he were about to say something but stopped.

"Tell me," Avelina pressed. "I would know the reason."

"Perhaps there is naught to tell."

"Before she passed"—Avelina crossed herself—"my mother said my ability to understand others was my greatest strength." Smiling, she added, "I believe 'tis my ability with the bow and arrow."

"Perhaps it is both. Will you show me?"

"Show you?"

"I was on my way to the training yard when. . ." He stopped.

"When?"

Niall's jaw clenched. His eyes narrowed just slightly.

She would not accept his reticence.

"When?" she prompted again.

"When I inquired as to your whereabouts and was told you were here."

Even knowing 'twas not likely a coincidence that Niall

had come to the garden, for him to confirm as much made her smile. In turn, he smiled back.

"Perhaps you will also tell me the story you held back earlier."

"You believe there is a story to tell?"

"I do."

"Hmm. Perhaps there is. And perhaps I will tell you, depending on your aim."

"Ahh, a contest, then?"

"Aye," he said as they began to walk side by side. "A contest."

"If I hit the bullseye in five tries—"

"Three."

She could do so in one. "Three," she confirmed. "You will tell me the story."

"I wished to visit the training yard this morn but did not."

"Then I am happy to accompany you."

She was happy for him to accompany her as well. After asking a servant to have the maid fetch her bow and arrow, they spoke of the hunt, of the inquiries the chieftain was making, but one thing they did not speak of as they made their way around the keep to the inner bailey was last eve's discussion.

Avelina could not raise the topic. What did one say? *Last eve, when we broached the subject of marriage, 'twas in jest, aye?*

Except, she had not been jesting. At least she had not last eve. So strong was her desire to be with him, Avelina would likely have agreed to their union. Which was as ridiculous a notion when she woke as it had been before. Her brother would never allow it. Her clansmen would not accept it. Nor would his, Avelina assumed. The chief's son and second-in-command simply did not marry a MacKinlay.

She knew it well.

And yet, as Niall spoke, she could not force thoughts of kissing him from her mind. Giving her virginity to a man she did not intend to marry might be, in this particular situation, less scandalous than the marriage alternative. But Avelina did not wish for that either.

"You are lost in thought," he said as they approached the training yard. The sounds of shouts and swords clashing reached their ears now, and Avelina was glad for Niall's presence. She'd never before trained anywhere but home.

"I am," she admitted, though could not admit the subject of those thoughts.

But perhaps he knew already, for as Niall gazed down at her, 'twas not difficult for her to think he might be having similar notions. In fact, she was sure of it.

Her heart raced.

Avelina's feet felt as if they were no longer on the ground. How dearly she wished for him to kiss her again.

With a low groan, a sound quite pleasing to her ears, he shook his head.

Somehow, she understood.

A longing. A frustration. A confusion she felt deeply as well.

Neither of them spoke again until they were in the training yard. Niall had spoken to one of the men and freed the target they would use. As if on cue, a young boy ran to them holding Avelina's bow and quiver up to her.

"I was asked to bring these to you, m'lady."

She thanked him, accepting the single carved bough bound in leather. Its string made from twisted sinews, the bow fit comfortably on her shoulder as Avelina removed an arrow. She wasted no time binding the arrowhead into a notch in the shaft, its barbs preventing premature withdrawal.

"Does it worry you that you're being watched?" he asked.

As she expected, it did not seem customary for a woman to be here in this yard. And indeed, Avelina was being watched. But with little else to occupy her—the standard pursuits of needlework and embroidery not of interest to her, and their household run smoothly by their steward who cared little for Avelina's interference—she'd taken to learning how to wield a bow and arrow.

Typically, in an actual training, Avelina would utilize a series of targets at varying distances set up on a range specifically designed for archery training. Today, however, she was not quite training but showing her skills. To a man she wanted to impress, even if she should not. That very man now backed away even as the crowd grew.

He'd given her three shots, but Avelina wanted to use just one.

At this distance, she could easily hit the center of the target. However, her pulse was not quite as steady as it should be. Closing her eyes, she forced herself not to think of him. His nearness or his visage. The look he'd given her back in the garden, as if he wanted to kiss her as much as Avelina wished it. She'd think of none of that.

Consider only the target.

She opened her eyes.

She ignored the spectators and focused solely on where she must hit. Naught else mattered. Her brother had told Avelina often that whatever she focused on would have her notice, and so she looked at just one spot.

Pulled back.

And released.

The moment Avelina's finger opened, she already knew the mark would be a hit. When it did, right in the center, she was little surprised. But apparently, most of her onlookers were, as they began to cheer and congratulate her.

"I suppose," a deep voice at her back said, "I owe you a story, lass?"

When she looked at him, Niall was actually smiling.

"I believe you do," she said, lowering her bow.

"Well then." He gestured for them to leave the training yard together. "Shall we find a private place to talk?"

A private place.

To talk.

Avelina took a deep breath, not daring to hope for more. And yet, her body knew what her mind refuted. It came alive, readying for their "talk," and Avelina was simply done fighting it.

CHAPTER
FIFTEEN

There were precious few places in most keeps for privacy, save a bedchamber, which was, in this instance, unacceptable. The next time Niall found himself alone with Lina in a bedchamber, he would damn well be making love to her.

Something he was not prepared to do.

She might be MacKinlay's sister, and some might be glad to see Niall defile her, but he was not that sort of man. Neither would his father condone such an action.

Having spied a small courtyard earlier on his way to the gardens, Niall led Lina there.

"Tell me how you learned to shoot so well?" he asked.

Though Niall may have expected she could use that bow Lina carried with her as they traveled, he'd not have expected her to use it so well. Few men could hit the center of a bullseye at that distance and even fewer in one try.

"When your father is killed, along with many of his men, and then your mother dies within a year of it, you do not wish to rely on others to protect you."

Lina said it too casually, as if she did not speak of the

death of her parents. He understood well her desire to protect herself from the pain, but Niall wondered also if she'd ever allowed herself to grieve.

"You say it as if you speak of the weather or some other mundane topic of conversation."

"I've become well accustomed to the fact."

Again, unlike the impassioned woman he'd spied many times these past days, this Lina was anything but. Rather than press her, Niall instead navigated her to a small courtyard between the bakehouse and the main keep.

Two stone benches would serve to keep them well enough apart.

Sitting, Niall adjusted his sword and looked up to see Lina gazing at him in a way that made him glad they were here and not in a bedchamber. He grew hard at her look, and only a deep breath, a readjustment of his position, and thoughts of battle—not the sort now occupying his mind but the kind his kinsmen did not return home from—helped reverse his discomfort.

"Your story," she said, reminding him that it was his story, not hers, that had been promised.

All in his clan knew of it, so 'twas no secret. Yet, he was reluctant to tell the tale to Lina. But Niall had promised.

"There is a healer on the outskirts of our village. For many years, she claimed to be visited by the devil. Even claimed to have played cards with him. Once, she'd said, the devil became so angry he'd lost that he tossed the table on which they played into a nearby lake. Despite the woman's skills as a healer, few believed her, of course."

He sighed, remembering. "As a jest, a friend and I began to visit her cottage in the eve. We would make noises outside her window. Pretend to be the very devil she claimed visited her."

"Devils, indeed," Lina said, smiling. She'd not be doing so when he finished his tale.

"One eve, she chased us. Tripped and twisted her ankle. An old woman even back then, 'twas an injury she never recovered from. Since that night, she has used a walking stick to aid her, the ankle not healing properly."

"How old were you?"

"I'd not yet seen ten summers."

"A boy, then."

"Aye. Even so. . ."

"This is why you smile so rarely?"

Niall shrugged. "Says my mother. Though, in truth, I do not remember a time that I smiled as often as my brother. The man sees good everywhere."

"But you do not?"

"I see it in some places. But I also see evil. Greed. Like you, I do not wish to relinquish control of my fate to others."

Lina looked down at her hands, which were folded atop her lap. When she looked up, 'twas not judgment he saw there but sadness.

Sadness for him.

"I doubt you were judged as harshly for something that occurred when you were a boy as you've judged yourself. Surely as a warrior you've ended men's lives?"

'Twas an abrupt change of topic.

"Indeed."

"Yet you mourn more for the healer's injury than for the wife or children of the men you've slain?"

"The two are very different. Warriors enter battle knowing they may not survive. They accept the consequences of their choice."

"Do men truly choose to become warriors or are they forced to do so to defend their family and clan?"

"'Tis both, I suppose."

"Whether the cause be just or unjust? Which makes me think of the healer."

He thought about that question for a time. At least, Niall attempted to concentrate on it. He found Lina's beauty, the soft lilting of her voice, quite distracting.

"Men may fight for a cause they find unjust, but their chief, or king, decrees otherwise. Though I do not understand how your question relates to the healer."

Lina blinked. "It does not, really. 'Twas simply a thought that occurred to me as we spoke."

Niall could not contain the bubble of laughter that formed in his stomach. He'd thought she was leading to some grand conclusion, but instead, Lina simply went round and round without necessarily returning to the beginning.

"You are a unique woman, Lina," he said. "I thought for certain you were looking for a way to assuage me from my guilt."

"If you've not been able to do it yourself after so many years, 'tis doubtful that would be a successful endeavor for me."

"Indeed," he agreed.

"So what, then, do you hope to accomplish with your questions?" Niall asked, curious.

"Just to get to know the man sitting across from me better."

"Because?" Niall allowed his vanity to ask the question.

Lina frowned, a rare sight for her. This time, it was she who was reluctant to speak.

"Why do you wish to get to know me better, Lina?" he asked again.

Sitting up a bit straighter, her chin rising, she looked him straight in the eye. "Because," she said, "I have decided there is a likelihood we will marry, and I would know my future husband before I commit to such a state."

Nothing, precisely nothing, could have prepared Niall for her decree.

Or for his body's reaction to the implication of her words.

CHAPTER
SIXTEEN

Surely, he misheard her.

"A likelihood," Niall repeated.

"Aye."

"The sister of the chief of Clan MacKinlay and the eldest son of the chief of Clan Duncraig?"

She nodded.

"Married."

Lina nodded again, this time with no hint of anything that might make Niall believe she jested with him.

Did he want to stand up from this bench, take Lady Avelina in his arms, kiss her, hold her, make love to her?

Aye, he did.

Even still...

"Do you understand the implications of your words?"

Lina did not hesitate. "I do. My brother will likely forbid it."

So, she did understand.

"And you would...?"

"Defy him."

"Defy him," he repeated. "Seems an extreme act, does it not?"

"Indeed. Yet I know my brother, and eventually, he would come to my side."

"And your clan?"

She sighed. "'Twould anger them, aye. But I believe you to be a good man, Niall. Mayhap, in time, others could see the same. Mayhap we could unite our clans with our union."

"You truly believe such a thing is possible? You see what havoc a few simple cattle wreak. Our feud's history is long, your slain too many in number for my ancestors to be forgiven, even though the battle was sanctioned."

"And yet, I am the daughter of one of those slain men."

"You could forgive me, but. . . could you forgive my father?" By her wince, he knew Lina's response. "As a married couple, we would live with my clan. I am to be the next chief."

She did not seem surprised by his declaration. Had she really given this matter some thought?

"Not an ideal arrangement, but one I would have to accept if I were to become your wife."

"Why would you even consider such a thing? Marry a man you hated just days ago. Whose family you still hate. Whose kinsman you may never come to accept."

Niall waited for her response.

"Because the way you look at me, the way you make me feel. . . 'tis the first time in all my life my body has come to life. The first time I felt anything as strongly as I feel a kinship to my brother or my friendship with my maid. I've been waiting for you, I think," she finished.

'Twas quite a declaration.

"What, precisely, do you feel for me, Lina?"

"A desire to stand up, come to you, sit beside you. Feel you next to me again. Not be far from you. When we ride, I wish to ride with you. When I sleep, I think of you. When I wake, 'tis your face I see before I even spy it."

He knew not what to say. "Your honesty is surprising."

Lina shrugged. "Should I say it is otherwise? Why pretend when you could be gone in days or sooner?"

She was right, of course. Though surprising, her honesty also pleased him. Niall would offer some of his own.

"What you feel is desire. I feel it too, Lina. More powerfully than I can ever remember before. I would say one does not marry for desire." Niall had to be careful with his words. "And yet..."

Niall had learned long ago that impetuousness could lead to dire consequences. Because of it, he'd learned to plan carefully. Make decisions based in logic. Which now held his tongue.

"Yet?" she pressed.

He let the silence between them linger as it must.

But then, she stood. Niall groaned at the vision of such a woman coming toward him. Groaned for the weakness that still resided in him, for as she sat beside him on the bench, he was now powerless. The air crackled between them. If they were caught in such an intimate manner...

But 'twas about to become even more so.

Mostly to dissuade himself, thinking the memory of their kiss must not be as powerful as Niall had made it in his mind, he leaned toward her. Lina met him halfway, and their lips touched. Gently at first. As if they were made for each other. But very quickly, the kiss spiraled.

Deepened.

He'd said one did not marry for desire, but if that ever

could be a basis for two people's union, this was the kind of kiss that could take them until the end of their days.

Never, not once, had Niall ever been sorry for the slain MacKinlay kinsmen. He'd been raised to hate the men who had long tortured his own. Stolen cattle, kidnappings, even murder if the tales were true.

But as he moved closer to Lina, deepening their kiss, his hand moving to sit atop her thigh, for the first time in his life he was sorry for the loss of her father. Likely, uncles and other relatives. Had they not fallen, perhaps her mother might not have gotten sick either.

Lina had been parentless, and she was here with her brother, showing a resilience that made him wish to deepen the kiss further.

To take her.

Make Lina his own.

Reluctantly, he pulled away.

Returned his hand to his own lap.

"Think on it more," Niall said. "What it would mean to come back to my home. Live among the men who slayed your kinsmen."

Her expressions, so serene just moments before, grew troubled. Though Lina had said she gave the matter consideration, he questioned just how deeply.

"My clan would not be pleased," she acknowledged. "And yours would likely not accept me."

It was true that they may not. "Think on it," he said.

"And you?"

Niall sighed. "I will do the same. For I can admit, Lina, my affection for you continues to grow. I, too, wish to be with you when we are apart. Kissing you, in some ways, is like torture because I wish for so much more. Yet, I am a practical man, too, and know the hurdles between us may be too difficult to cross."

Her smile could make a hardened warrior weep.

"I'd not have taken you for a man who gives much concern to hurdles."

"'Twould be foolish to ignore them."

"Ignore? Nay. See them as unsurmountable? Perhaps you are not the man I thought you were." She moved to stand.

He grabbed her wrist and pulled her back down.

He looked into her eyes. "Your instincts are correct, my lady. I take what I want, but in this instance, what I want may be at odds with what's best for my clan."

"And clan above all?"

"For a man who would be chief? Aye."

She seemed resigned, if not pleased, by the notion. "Of course." Lina stood.

He did the same. "I do not wish you to be ashamed for telling me what you have today."

"Ashamed? Why should I be ashamed for sharing what is in my heart?"

She was like no other noblewoman he knew. "Indeed, you should not."

"Fortune favors the bold, Niall. You must believe that."

"I do."

"Then it seems we both have much thinking to do."

He smiled. "It seems you are right. In the meantime, shall I escort you to the battlements? I wished to view the landscape around the keep. Perhaps you'd do so with me?"

Though he would very much wish instead to remain here, continuing to kiss this beautiful, passionate woman as he had last night, Niall found his discipline faltering a bit with her. Finding themselves in a more public place would serve him well.

"I would enjoy that," she said.

He resisted the urge to reach down for her hand. Avelina MacKinlay was not his, and Niall had no claim over her. He wished he did.

And perhaps, in time, he just might.

CHAPTER
SEVENTEEN

They spotted the riding party at the same time.

"It seems we have been up here for overly long," Avelina said.

First, she and Niall had stood in one spot, always with guards watching. They'd talked of their childhoods. Of their families. Avelina told Niall of her maid, her friends, and her fervent wish that her brother would find someone to love. His heart had become hardened since their father's death, the carefree, young boy she remembered as a child not the one who rode toward the keep even now.

Eventually, they walked the length of the battlements, never touching, though coming close. Avelina could feel the heat of him at times. She could smell the scent that was uniquely his, one that spoke of a recent bath with the scent of sandalwood reaching her nose. They did not speak again of marriage, or even of their own relations, but instead of their pasts.

And eventually, just before the riding party appeared, their futures.

Niall had asked what Avelina had dreamed of for her

future, and she'd been about to tell him that dream had been very recently altered since meeting him. But she had not, the moment passed, and they were about to be set upon by their host and Avelina's brother.

"We should descend before he spots us," she said.

Niall did not move however.

"You do not wish him to see us together, yet you are willing to tell your brother you wish to marry me?"

"To incur his wrath for our union, aye, I am willing to do so. But to incur it for a conversation?" She shrugged.

"Avelina," he said just as she was about to turn toward the stone steps. His tone gave her pause. "You would truly wish to marry me? To return with me to Duncraig?"

A madness overtook her that Avelina could not explain. How long had she tried to force herself from her brother's shadow? To define what it was, precisely, that she wished for? That dream Niall asked about? It had never been clear to her before. A husband, surely. But Avelina could not summon a man's face in her mind. Certainly, she had never met someone to inspire an urgent desire to marry.

Until now.

Her greatest enemy.

"I do not wish to reside at Duncraig," she admitted. "But neither do I wish to be parted from you. Or not know your kiss, or more, ever again." Avelina surprised herself with her forthrightness. But 'twas true, and so she said it despite feeling as if she had just opened her chest and laid her heart bare to a man she barely knew.

"Do you not wish to marry for love?"

Avelina was not so naive as that. "I do not expect it."

"Unusual for a—"

"A woman?"

"Aye."

Avelina chose not to take offense. "Perhaps. But I am practical." The sound of the riding party coming closer told Avelina they'd likely already been spotted here. Rushing down the stairs now would be of little use.

Neither of them moved. Avelina had surprised herself, and though she wanted to look away, she would not. Instead, she met Niall's gaze, which she was unfortunately unable to decipher.

"I do not wish to be parted from you either," he said finally. "And would very much like to know your kiss again." Suddenly, Avelina did know his thoughts. Gone was the hardened look of a warrior, replaced by the very sensual one of a man. "And much more."

"Niall," a voice called from below.

They both looked down to the courtyard at the same time. 'Twas his brother who was now gesturing for him, or both of them, to join him.

With a sigh, Niall held out his hand, and Avelina took it, stepping down and relinquishing his hold only when forced to do so as she descended the stairs.

"Your presence is being requested in the hall," Niall's brother said with a look of disapproval. Avelina did not take offense.

She understood. Knew her own brother would do the same.

"Shall we?" Niall asked her as all three of them made their way through the busy courtyard toward the entrance of the hall.

Attempting to calm her rapidly beating heart, Avelina focused instead on the brother, who was looking up at the keep with a most curious expression.

"You seem troubled, my lord."

"I've told my brother there is something. . . familiar about this keep," Kieran said.

"Yet you've not been here before."

"Nay," he said, turning his attention to her. "I am certain. I've not."

They were very different, the two men. Everything about the brother was darker—his hair, his eyes. . . all but his smile, which came easier than Niall's.

By the time they entered the hall, the servants had begun to prepare for the evening meal. Avelina truly had not realized she and Niall had been together for so long. It seemed to her 'twas no time at all.

Her own brother sat just in front of the high table, where their host spoke to a serving maid. When the chieftain saw them enter the hall, he gestured for them to sit.

With her brother.

Niall balked, of course, stopping in his tracks. Neither did Avelina's brother seem pleased, but they were guests here, and Tannochbrae was doing them a favor by investigating the matter of their cattle, so Avelina shot her brother a glare.

'Twas not often he heeded her, but at this moment, at least, he softened his expression.

"Come," she whispered to Niall, "sit with me."

At the foot of the table, a serving maid held out a bowl with lilac-scented water, which each of them, in turn, used to wash their hands. Then, sitting beside her brother, who spoke with a man Avelina had never seen before, she watched as Niall and his brother sat across from them, ignoring Ewan and speaking quietly to each other.

Eventually, however, the inevitable occurred. Her brother finished his conversation and focused on Niall.

"The chieftain wishes to speak with us after the meal," he said, his tone curt.

"Has he discovered anything of import?"

Her brother shrugged. "If he did, I do not know of it yet."

Silence.

"How was your hunt, Brother?" Avelina asked.

"We will taste the rewards of our hunt this eve," he said. Which meant it had gone well.

"Tannochbrae said nothing of the cattle?" Kieran asked.

Ewan answered nay, followed by more questions from Niall's brother, each of which, along with their answers, was as terse as the last.

She caught Niall's gaze. He seemed disinterested in the men's conversation but very interested in her. Avelina's pulse quickened. The conversation was as uncomfortable as her insides, which swirled about every time Niall looked at her. Though the feeling was less of a discomfort than it was. . . something else.

An impossible situation, this. The hatred at this table was as palatable as the affection she'd begun to bear for Niall. Finally, and to her dismay, her brother addressed the one topic Avelina would have hoped to avoid.

"You and my sister," he said, as if she were not sitting just next to him.

When he did not finish, Niall asked innocently, "Aye?"

"I should have known better than to leave the two of you alone at the keep."

Avelina cared not that her brother's nostrils flared—a clear indication he was angry.

"I am sitting just beside you," she said. "And can speak to whomever I please."

"Why you would wish to, knowing what he's done—"

"What his clan has done. Niall was just a boy."

Her brother's harsh laugh cut off the remainder of her words. "Niall? So, you are using his given name?"

"Avelina," Niall said, a direct response to her brother's displeasure at her using Niall's given name, "may surely choose with whom to speak and with whatever level of familiarity she chooses."

Her brother stood.

Niall did the same.

Avelina sighed.

'Twas inevitable, surely. However. . . "Not in our host's hall," she said, aware they were now very much the center of attention.

Their host held his hand before him, gesturing that the two men should sit.

"He gives us aid," Kieran said, "which surely we need to learn what truly has been happening with these cattle. Would you get us thrown from the hall because you cannae conduct a civil conversation?"

He seemed to address his brother just as much as her own.

Neither man said a word.

Finally, as Avelina held her breath waiting, they began to sit at the same time.

"Keep my sister's name from your mouth," her brother added.

Avelina rolled her eyes. "Ewan," she warned.

"I make no promises," Niall said in response.

Despite it, the meal passed in relative peace, until the chieftain stood at the end of the meal and summoned all four of them to his private chamber. Escorted from the hall and to his solar chamber not far from it, Avelina said a silent prayer no argument had broken out.

That was, until the chieftain welcomed the men but stopped her at the doorframe.

"I am certain they will send word to you, my lady, when our conversation is finished."

To which Niall replied, "There will be no need as Lady Avelina will join us."

Her brother seethed.

Tannochbrae bristled.

For her part, Avelina said nothing. Gave nothing away by her expression. But knew one thing for certain. In choosing Niall, she'd not made a mistake.

CHAPTER
EIGHTEEN

"No, Niall, do not."

Of course, his brother had heard him. The man was a better tracker than any other. He heard everything. Probably felt Niall rise from his bed.

Reaching for his sword, he said nothing. Fastening it to his belt, his boots on already, he once again found himself having a late-night discussion with Kieran.

"I must."

She was fire.

She was life.

Watching her in that meeting with the chieftain, Niall could not imagine any other but her by his side. As Tannochbrae had described what he'd learned thus far—the most interesting fact being that the cattle were seen by the blacksmith's apprentice, who had been hunting with some of the boys from the village, being led east by a man he did not know—she'd remained quiet. But when he insisted there was naught else that could be done, Lina refused to let the matter drop. Even when both he and her brother agreed with the chieftain and thanked him for his efforts.

"There are none on that path who might know more? No dwellings close to the border? Surely there is someone who can identify the man who, we can likely all agree, wishes to reignite a war between our clans?"

"Perhaps you should look to your own clan, my lady, as the cattle are yours?"

Niall had thought to intervene, not caring for the man's tone toward Lina.

She did not give him the opportunity. "As we most certainly are doing, my lord. But surely you need no reminder of the consequences of a renewed war between Clans Duncraig and MacKinlay."

Tannochbrae lands lay between them, and if history was any sort of teacher, the lesson was simple. They would be as affected as anyone. The king would not have intervened all those years ago if their clans could have made some sort of peace on their own. If their feud had not affected so many of their neighbors.

"Of course, I was but a girl, so perhaps I am wrong," she had finished.

Niall, unable to resist, had laughed aloud, incurring glares both from their host and Lina's brother. Even now, he smiled in the darkness thinking of the exchange.

Their host had agreed to send a messenger to "one who may have seen the cattle's movement." Which meant a few more days in this keep. Ones Niall now intended to take full advantage of.

'Twas inevitable, he and Lina. He would go to her. Tell her as much.

Kiss her. Make love to her.

Marry her.

Perhaps she was right. Their union may even unite their clans. They were nearly neighbors, and there was no doubt both clans would be stronger as allies. None could deny it. Of course, neither would most likely accept it. His father would be furious. His mother, less likely so.

"You will marry her?" His brother sat up in his bed.

"I will."

"Father will not accept her. Neither will our clansman."

Niall took a candle and its holder from the table and brought it toward the wall torch. Lighting it, he moved toward his brother.

"Will you?"

Kieran sighed heavily. "My approval means little."

He looked into his brother's eyes, the candlelight dancing in them. His brother's love, adoration even, was not something Niall ever questioned. Nor did he do so now.

"Will you?" he asked again.

"Aye, of course. That you would ask such a question—"

"You've been opposed to us from the start."

"Because it will be a difficult path for you and for her. What do you believe our clansman will say if you return to Duncraig with a MacKinlay as a wife? 'Twill be difficult for her, Niall."

"I know it well," he replied. "Lina does too. But. . ." How to describe a feeling he'd never had before now? "When I am with her, I can breathe easily. When I am not, I think of her. Wish for her to be near. I cannae explain it properly, Brother. There are no words I can give you other than the ones I already offer."

"There is a word, Brother. And you know it well."

He shook his head. "We've not known each other for long."

"And yet, it does not seem to matter, does it? When two people are meant for each other."

"I do not believe in that."

Kieran laughed. "It matters not if you believe in love, Niall, to feel it. What you describe is certainly your love for Avelina MacKinlay."

Kieran would know as his brother had been deeply in love with a woman once. All had thought they would marry. "You believe it to be so?"

"Indeed."

"Perhaps I'd not been in love before as I once thought. This is a feeling I'd not ask for if given the choice. 'Tis much too powerful."

"And yet, it seems you were not. If there is any woman you should not love, 'tis the very one you seek this night."

They were silent for a moment and then Kieran asked softly, "You are certain?"

"I am certain," Niall said.

"Then go to her. We will consider the consequences on the morrow. And when we return home with Lady Avelina by your side. In the meantime. . ." Kieran was as passionate a man as any. His brother smiled. "Enjoy your evening, Brother."

Niall thought of what it had felt like for Lina to be in his arms, her lips and his joined.

"I intend to, Brother," he said. "I intend to."

CHAPTER
NINETEEN

Somehow, she knew he would come.

He'd not told her as much. When they parted, it was with barely a word as her brother whisked her from the solar chamber to "speak with you on multiple matters." Her outburst to their host. She and Niall. If there was anything she did that Ewan took kindly to, it was certainly not on this trip. She loved him and despised him all at once. If only Ewan would be her brother and not attempt to be her father too.

Avelina knew not where Niall slept, but neither would it matter, since he'd mentioned sharing a bedchamber with his brother. Instead, she made use of the hot bath that had been sent to her. With a fresh shift and her hair braided courtesy of the maid, Avelina should have been prepared for bed.

Instead, she stood before the fire, her toes wiggling into the fur rug under her feet, the slippers she'd brought staying unused for now. And when the knock at her door pulled Avelina out of her reverie, she was not at all surprised.

Glad, aye.

Excited, also. But surprised? Nay. Something had shifted between them that eve. So when she opened the door as she had the night before, allowing Niall inside, nothing was more natural than to fall into his arms the moment the door closed. His hands were everywhere at once, grasping the material at her buttocks. Squeezing them, along with fistfuls of her shift, Niall pulled her hips toward him as their lips came together as naturally as if they were made to kiss one another.

When he groaned, Avelina sighed, pulling Niall even closer. He guided them closer to the fire, for which she was grateful, and the chill from under her door no longer crept up her legs. Instead, 'twas warm, even as he lifted her shift up, breaking the kiss. She wore nothing under it, so when her arms lifted to aid him, and Niall pulled it over her head, for the first time in her entire life, Avelina was nude in front of a man.

Yet, oddly, she felt neither shame nor embarrassment.

"By God and his disciples, Lina, you are perfectly made." Niall removed his sword, still staring at her. "Your breasts are magnificent."

He removed his boots next, but instead of disrobing further, Niall came to her once more. He cupped both breasts, and she thought he meant to kiss her. Instead, he lowered his head and kissed her chest, and then both breasts. Moving to one, he trailed more kisses toward her nipple and then took her into his mouth.

As he suckled, his teeth grazing her, Lina still felt no shame. The sensations that arose in her were much too pleasant for such a thing. "Niall," she said, her hands moving toward his head, grasping his hair with them both. "Please," she begged, knowing not what she asked for.

He moved to the other breast, giving it as complete attention as the first.

And then he knelt before her. With the fire before them and Niall below her, Lina was only temporarily confused until she realized his intentions. Never had she heard of such a thing.

"Niall?"

But he would not be waylaid. Lifting one of her legs and placing her foot on his bent knee, he glanced up at her briefly, smiled, and touched her most intimate spot. Not just touched it, but used his thumbs to part her.

"What do you mean to—"

His head bent toward her. Surely he would not...

Kiss her there? Nay, not kiss her. Niall's tongue swept her, more like a lick than a kiss.

There. Right on her most private area.

Surely this was not a thing people did. And yet, with his fingers holding her open for him, Niall continued to lick. To suckle. And then one of his thumbs pressed just above his lips and began to circle.

Lina's fingers wrapped around his hair as if she meant to hold on. Which, in fact, she did. Because with the things Niall was doing to her now, Lina began to have some difficulty standing.

Her knees would surely give way at any moment.

"Niall," she called out in between the other sounds escaping from her lips. Ones she'd never made before. "Please," she begged him as he continued. But now his movements were slower, more deliberate. At least, his tongue swirled slowly as his thumb pressed more quickly.

"I cannae," she said, hardly understanding her own words. "I must let go," she added, realizing now 'twas precisely what she wanted. To forget the fact that a man who was neither her husband nor her betrothed knelt before her, between her legs, with his lips and tongue on her most intimate parts of her body.

He pulled from her. "Let go, love. Listen to your body and let everything go."

Love.

'Twas nothing more than an endearment, but it made Avelina's heart skip a beat nonetheless. But then she had no more time to think. His mouth was on her again, and this time, Niall did not relent at all. It was if all of him covered all of her, the suckling something she wasn't sure she could continue standing for. But somehow, she managed to as her legs began to shake, her core clenching.

Avelina called out Niall's name as the pulses began and then continued. Her hands tightened in his hair as the pulses came, wave after wave. Breathing heavily, she felt as if her entire body were engulfed in that fire as the waves began to ebb.

When Niall stood up, Avelina was certain watching him wipe his lips with his fingers, the secret smile on his face just for her, was the single most pleasurable thing she'd ever seen. But certainly not the most pleasurable thing she'd ever felt.

The prize for that went to what Niall had just done to her.

"I'd not been expecting that," Avelina said as Niall reached for her.

"I would not have thought you would, but I wanted to give you a taste of what will be between us."

His arms were around her now, and Avelina had to look up to meet his gaze.

"Between us," she repeated, feeling quite bare against his clothed chest.

"Aye." Niall leaned down to kiss her, gently, before standing back up. "You know why I am here this eve. Do you not?"

"I do," she said, still marveling at what he'd done.

"If we are to make love this eve, you will be my wife, Lina."

"Aye," she agreed. She'd not give herself to him otherwise.

"You are prepared for that?"

"Nay," she said. "Of course I am not. You are a Duncraig. The Duncraig's eldest son and second to your chief."

His finger moved under her chin, lifting it. "Avelina?"

"Aye, Niall?"

"Are you prepared to become my wife? Will you marry me, lass?"

She was going to ask if she'd allow his face to be buried between her legs otherwise but thought better of it. This was the moment for brevity, not glibness.

"I am. And I will."

Niall kissed her then, a kiss full of promise. Full of, dare she think it, hope.

And before she knew it, Avelina was being lifted into the air and carried to the bed. She was about to lose her virginity, something she had guarded carefully her entire life.

And was now giving it to her greatest enemy.

CHAPTER TWENTY

He vowed to go slowly with her, but Niall simply could not stop touching every bit of this woman's body. She was so perfectly formed. Her breasts, her hips. The taste of her still on his lips.

Laying her down on the bed, Niall removed his clothing piece by piece, watching as Lina pushed down the coverlet and climbed under it. She watched him in apparent fascination, Niall waiting for her reaction when he removed his plaid and, finally, the tunic under it. He would not preen like a schoolboy at her expression.

"Niall," she exclaimed as he climbed into the bed with her.

Tearing the coverlet down, he moved between her legs once again. Kneeling, he smiled as she continued to look at him.

"That cannae possibly go inside me."

"It can, lass, and 'twill be pleasure for us both, I can assure you."

Still, she shook her head. And since Niall did not wish

for her to worry, he distracted her by running his hands up both of her legs. Between her thighs then, he used his thumbs to massage the soft flesh there. Then, pushing her legs open, he bent between them once more.

"Niall."

He saw her grasp the coverlet with both hands balled into fists just as he began to lick, to entice. 'Twas working wondrously well, his beautiful, former enemy so wet so quickly. Her response to him was something Niall could have predicted. Lina was as passionate in the bedchamber as she was outside it.

"Niall," she called again.

In response, he pulled away and moved between her legs, ready to make this woman his. But he would be certain first.

"If we do this—"

"We are bound together, aye."

Her knees bent, Lina's braid hanging down her chest... she looked so damn perfect, Niall nearly came at that moment just gazing at her.

Overcome with the need to claim her, waiting in that breath as long as one did before being rushed during a battle, he finally watched as Lina smiled into the darkness, the candle and distant light of the fire the only thing illuminating her.

"I would not part from you," she repeated the refrain from the battlements.

Neither would he wish to part from her. And so, Niall moved between her legs and positioned himself, slipping just the very tip of him inside her.

"'Twill hurt but a moment, I am told," he said. "Though I do not make a practice of taking women's virginity, so I cannae say for certain."

Lina blinked, clearly worried. But she underestimated how easily he would slip inside her, courtesy of a wetness that made it difficult to go slowly. He did, however, pushing ever so gently until he was pressed against her barrier.

Leaning down atop her, careful not to crush her, Niall groaned as his chest made contact with her breasts. Inhaling the sweet scent of her, he lowered his head to her, kissing Lina thoroughly, his tongue swirling and touching hers until, without warning, he broke through.

Avelina was a virgin no longer.

She stilled, as did he. But Niall never stopped kissing her, and she responded in kind. He wanted to ask her if it hurt but could not stopping kissing the woman. Thankfully, she gave what likely would have been her answer as her hips began to move.

Niall moved with the rhythm of her hips. Slowly, at first, and then faster. Pressing his hand between their bodies, he rubbed the spot that would make her call out his name, and sure enough, her hips bucked off the bed, but he did not stop.

His tongue matched their movements below. Niall was determined for Lina's first time to be nothing less than the kind of lovemaking she'd be thinking of every waking moment on the morrow.

She broke their kiss then, looking at him in wonder as her fingers clutched both of his arms. "I never imagined," she began, stopping as he slowed his movements and began to circle his hips.

Lina moved with him.

"I want you to come for me," he said. At her confused expression, he added, "As you did before the fire. I want you to find release before I spill my seed in you." Niall held her gaze. "You are mine now, Lina. Do you understand?"

She nodded. "As you are mine."

He was and would prove it. Thrusting harder now, he rode her until Lina grabbed him with everything she had and dug her nails into his arms. "Niall," she said, as he circled and rubbed, thrusting now relentlessly.

"Lina," he said. "Come for me, love. Come all over my cock."

"Oh," she said, perhaps a bit shocked by his words. Eyes wide, lips open, she made a sound that told him she was close.

"Come for me, Lina. Let it go."

"I am, Niall. I am," she said, and sure enough, there was even more wetness than before. With a final few thrusts, he came with her, exploding into this woman who was now his—if not his wife yet.

Burying himself in her, Niall collapsed against her, ensuring he did not crush her in the process. Lying with his face buried in her neck, still inside her, Niall closed his eyes, hardly able to believe he had just taken Lady Avelina of MacKinlay's innocence after declaring his intention to make her his wife.

Wife.

Husband.

A word that did not terrify him as it once had. Yet a title he felt little worthy of. A man such as him, one who was in all likelihood incapable of love, his actions too measured for such an emotion... yet worse than that for Lina.

She was a MacKinlay.

She would not have an easy time of it at Duncraig Castle.

Lifting his head, Niall kissed her neck, still not willing to move from her. "I would stay inside you all eve," he said, kissing her everywhere his lips would reach.

"I would welcome it."
As would he.

CHAPTER
TWENTY-ONE

She was supposed to have waited for Niall, but after pacing her chamber for what felt like the entire morn, Avelina finally decided to confront her brother herself. He would be finished breaking his fast by now, something she would have done, too, had she not still been abed.

With her betrothed.

They'd said the words that made the fact official and would wed that very day. A grand wedding between a Duncraig and MacKinlay would be nothing more than a breeding ground for fighting. When Niall first asked if she would consider marrying straightaway, she'd agreed immediately.

What was done, was done. She'd given herself to him, and 'twas no use waiting. Besides, they would not stay here much longer and would be parting ways soon enough. Unless, of course, they were wed.

Which they would be. Today.

'Twas madness, surely. But for once, Avelina had made a choice that was for herself, not her brother or clan. And there was a peace that came with knowing Niall and she would not be parted. Then, of course, there was what he'd done to her last eve.

As she made her way to the hall, her cheeks flushed with the memory of their lovemaking. Three times he'd entered her, the first of which had been painful for a time, but even then she'd eventually found great pleasure. The other two times... Avelina smiled.

"Pardon," she said to a serving maid, "I am looking for my brother."

"The MacKinlay chief?" she asked, already looking toward her lord's solar chamber where they'd met the day before.

"Aye," she said, and the maid led her from the hall, which was mostly empty.

"This way."

When they arrived, the maid, without authority to enter, said she would fetch the steward to allow them entry.

"There is no need," Avelina said, knocking on the thick wooden door with her knuckles.

"My lady..." The poor maid appeared appalled.

Avelina knocked again. This time, the chieftain himself opened the door. So, no servant to do so? He was perhaps less pretentious than Avelina had first thought him to be.

Her brother was, indeed, inside.

"Pardon the interruption, my lord. But I would speak to my brother on an urgent matter if it pleases you."

The chieftain gestured for her to come inside. "Of course, my lady."

Since this matter affected him as well, she blurted out the words that had been swirling in her mind all morn to both men. "Niall has gone to speak to Tannochbrae's priest. We'd planned to speak with you both afterward, but. . ." She saw the chieftain sit from the corner of her eye, but Avelina watched her brother's reaction. "We will be married at once."

She need not have watched him so closely for his reaction. Her brother shot up from his chair and, for all of Tannochbrae to hear, shouted precisely the words she expected.

"You will not marry that man."

Avelina sighed. "I will, Brother. We—"

"I forbid it. You cannae," he said to the chieftain, "host a wedding I, as chief, forbid."

"Nay," he agreed. "I cannae."

He was about to change his mind. "I am no longer a maid," she told her brother, Unsuccessfully willing her cheeks not to redden. "So, aye, I will be marrying him."

Avelina had never before seen her brother this angry. She'd expected it, of course, but 'twas still disagreeable to witness him in such a state.

"You," he sputtered. "He. . ." Apparently, her brother could not speak.

So, she turned to their host instead. "I do apologize for any inconvenience this may cause you, my lord. But would like to assure you, before my brother questions me further on the matter, I was very much a willing participant in the matter."

The chieftain looked from her to her brother, his expression a combination of surprise and amusement.

"The matter," he repeated.

"Aye. Of the loss of my virginity."

"Lina." Her brother finally found his voice. "You speak of such things as if they are a trivial matter. We've discussed your marriage many times."

"And many times I've told you I have no interest in marriage."

"Until now. With—" He struggled to compose himself. "The second to the clan chief of Duncraig. The son of the man who murdered your father. Your uncle."

Before Ewan could continue, she said, "As I've stated before, Brother, he did not participate in that battle. Niall killed no one. And 'twas no murder besides. It was a battle sanctioned by the king of Scotland."

"The lass speaks true," the chieftain added. "And 'twas many years ago. Perhaps with this union, your clans can find a way to unite. MacKinlay and Duncraig as allies would make this region as formidable as any. 'Tis a fine plan indeed."

"A fine plan," her brother spat. "Nay, 'tis not a fine plan, as she—" He turned to her. "You will not be marrying Duncraig."

As if on cue, the door opened. No knock. No steward's announcement. Precisely the easy way she'd have imagined Niall might enter the room.

He must have heard her brother's shouting through the door. Niall walked up to her, took Avelina's hand, squeezed it, and said, quite clearly, "She will, either with none but the priest as witness or, if my lord wills it. . ." He turned to the chieftain. "Tomorrow, as a celebration of two neighboring clans forming a union here in your hall, something that can only benefit Clan Tannochbrae. Either way, the priest agrees the union must be done." Niall gave his attention to her brother then. "Assuming you know the state of your sister's maidenhood already."

Every part of her brother wanted to come for Niall. She could see his hands twitching, yet Ewan would not draw his sword in this chamber. The offense to their host would be too great.

"You took what was not yours to take," her brother seethed.

She did not wish for Ewan to be upset but neither could she back down from this decision.

"I gave it freely, Ewan," she said softly. "You've known of my affection for him."

"Known and warned against it."

"It seems your warning was not heeded." The chieftain sighed. "They will marry either way under these conditions. I would have it be a cause for celebration and will gladly host the wedding feast on the morrow."

"Wedding feast," her brother muttered. "There should not be a wedding."

But there would be, and he knew it. By giving herself to Niall, Avelina had guaranteed it. Letting go of Niall's hand, she closed the distance between her and her brother. Taking both of his hands in hers, now that the surprise had worn off, Avelina attempted to reach him.

"'Tis of my choosing, Brother. An alliance, perhaps, that may benefit our clan. But either way, 'tis done. I care for him and knew you'd not accept him otherwise."

"I do not accept him now."

It was as she expected, even if Avelina had hoped for more. "You do not give this marriage your blessing?"

"I do not." His answer was immediate.

Squeezing her brother's hands, she dropped them, but made her intentions clear by moving back to Niall's side. Taking his hand once again, exchanging glances with the man who would be her husband on the morrow, she said to the chieftain, "We will gladly accept your offer of a wedding feast and look forward to a cause to celebrate as we await further word about the cattle."

"Then it appears there is much to be done," Tannochbrae said with a final glance at Ewan. "I am sorry for it, MacKinlay, but he has taken from her that which cannae be repaired except through matrimony."

"He did not take it," Avelina said, though none seemed to listen. She looked up at Niall, who smiled for the first time since coming into the chamber.

A smile that said, "Aye, lass. I did. And would do it again."

She'd just angered her brother, informed their host there would be a wedding at Tannochbrae tomorrow, and agreed to wed a man whose people would likely not accept her. Despite it, Avelina had just one thought as Niall looked at her in that way.

And it had naught to do with the wedding. Or their host. Or her brother.

But only of... the wedding bed.

CHAPTER
TWENTY-TWO

He'd not seen her since last eve's meal.

Yesterday had been quite a day, from the confrontation in Tannochbrae's solar chamber to a visit with a merchant having just returned from the very area where MacKinlay's cattle had been grazing. After learning the man knew naught, as expected, Niall spent the afternoon training as Avelina and Tannochbrae's seamstress worked on a gown the chieftain insisted on commissioning.

The man had taken to this wedding nearly as much as he and Avelina. The idea of two neighbors being allies instead of enemies was one he clearly relished. In the chieftain's mind, 'twould make their region as formidable as any, and while that might be true, he regretted to inform the man this union was unlikely to bring swift changes to their clans' relations.

As evidenced by Avelina's brother's reaction.

Or even his own brother, who continued to worry for the reception Avelina would receive upon returning to Castle Duncraig.

Finally, at the evening meal, he'd had an opportunity to see her. They sat, as requested by their host, together on either side of the host, a place of honor, surely. But they'd not had the opportunity for a private discussion.

Niall was further dismayed to learn Avelina would not be sleeping alone that eve. As per custom, she would be attended by a maid to ensure the precise thing he'd been looking forward to all day, being inside Avelina once again.

It was not to be, however, and he'd made do with a quick stolen kiss in the corridor and promise of more on the morrow. On his wedding day.

He stood now beside his brother in the Tannochbrae chapel, waiting for sounds of the piper who would announce Avelina's arrival.

"You are truly getting married today," Kieran said beside him. "I'd not believe it were I not standing here beside you."

"I know you do not agree, but I cannae explain it, Kieran. 'Tis the right decision."

"I dinnae agree or disagree. 'Tis your decision, Brother, and I stand by you as you make it."

Niall put his hand on his brother's shoulder. Kieran placed his own over Niall's.

"You are the best brother a man could have," he said sincerely.

"As are you, Niall. I would say this," he added, dropping his hand. "I've not seen you smile so often as you have since meeting Lady Avelina."

He listened but still heard no pipers. There were few in the chapel with them since most stood outside waiting for the bride to arrive. But he could not see her until she entered the building, so Niall and Kieran stood, alone, together.

"I told her of the healer," he said, the words coming to him at the very moment he said them.

As expected, his brother seemed surprised. Niall never spoke of it with good reason.

"And still, she is marrying you," Kieran teased. His brother had always thought Niall berated himself too often about it.

"'Twas cruel," he said, remembering.

"You were a boy," Kieran said. "And now a man about to become a husband."

A husband.

The sound, distinct but distant, was one that filled Niall with both joy and sorrow. Joy for he knew this decision to be the right one. Sorrow for not being wed with his parents and relatives in attendance. His mother would be especially disappointed, but neither could he traipse about the countryside having taken Avelina's virginity and not rectify the fact. Besides, he would not be apart from her for even one more night.

"She's coming," his brother stated what they both knew well. The pipers' joyful melody became louder and louder, the crowd that gathered—one who knew neither he nor the bride—began to cheer. Here in the Highlands, a wedding was cause for celebration no matter the couple.

Niall waited for what seemed like a full day until, finally, the chapel began to fill. When the door finally fully cleared, he stared at it.

And then she appeared. Alone, as her brother had refused to attend their wedding.

A simple, deep blue gown, ironic as blue symbolized purity, and he knew better than anyone in attendance what had occurred between him and Avelina two nights ago. He'd thought of little else since, but now was not the time to lust after his wife. They had to make it through the ceremony and wedding feast first.

With her hair piled atop her head, Niall had never in his life seen anything more beautiful than his intended walking toward him.

When she reached up to the altar, Niall took her hand and pulled Lina to his side. Perhaps too close since the priest, now before them, gave him a look that said as much, but Niall did not care. He listened to the words the priest spoke, remembered how to use his tongue as they exchanged wedding bands and vows, and somehow, Niall managed to get to the part where he could kiss his bride.

He kissed her, indeed. So long that the priest cleared his throat, those in attendance cheered, and Avelina actually pulled away, likely embarrassed by the extension of the kiss. But he cared only to keep his new bride as close to him as possible, never releasing her elbow at his side even when surrounded by well-wishers outside the chapel.

"We are married," she whispered to him. "Well and truly wed."

"Indeed, we are," he said, kissing her on the cheek, enduring jests for his displays of affection because of it. "And if I will be tormented for a quick kiss on the cheek," he said to her, "then I will do so for more than a peck."

Taking his wife's face in his hands, Niall kissed her thoroughly, prompting more cheers.

"I'd not have taken you for a man of affection in front of so many." Avelina waved her arm to indicate the crowd.

He leaned toward her ear. "I'd not have taken you to be a screamer in bed, my lady wife, but here we are."

Her mouth opened wide in surprise. "I did not scream," she said only for his ears.

"But you will," he promised.

Lina's mouth still open, Niall laid the pad of his finger on her lips to close it, winking at her. If this exchange were any indication, he would enjoy being a husband to Lina.

"You are no gentleman, husband," she said, as if testing the word.

"Nor did I claim to be," he said, their conversation cut off by the chieftain himself. He'd apparently just emerged from the chapel.

"I am sorry your brother did not join us," the chief said to Avelina.

"As am I," she said, clearly meaning the words.

They both looked at Niall, but he had nothing to add. He was only sorry for it inasmuch as it pained Lina. For himself, Niall was glad to be free of the MacKinlay's presence.

"But now," Tannochbrae said, turning to the crowd. "We celebrate the union of two clans, neighbors and allies of Tannochbrae, with a feast. All," he shouted to the gathered crowd. "Are welcome."

More cheers greeted his words after Niall finally remembered his manners. "I failed to tell you how beautiful you look today, lady wife."

Her smile was Niall's reward, and the only one he needed.

"And I've a surprise under this gown for you, my esteemed husband. But you must wait for this eve to see it."

They looked at one another. "A surprise?"

"Indeed."

"I think I will not wait for it," he said, surprising her in return by scooping Lina into his arms as he'd done two nights before when carrying her to bed. This time, though, he might not be able to whisk the woman into

Tannochbrae's keep and into her bedchamber, he had other plans.

"To the hall," he said, the crowd clearly enjoying their display.

And though they followed, he had no intention of taking Lina directly to the hall. He'd see his wife's surprise, one he'd discover now, and Niall knew precisely where to do it.

CHAPTER
TWENTY-THREE

After calling back to the crowd that they would meet them in the hall, Niall turned toward the gardens where they'd had that first discussion. Though it was empty, when he put her down and looked at her in a way that left nothing to interpretation, Avelina shook her head.

"Nay, we cannae. Someone may come into the gardens and see us."

He navigated them to a path behind the tallest trees in the gardens, but even so, they would have little warning were someone to come upon them.

"You are my wife," Niall said, pulling her into his arms. "If they see us, so be it."

Avelina looked to the entrance of the gardens. "What if—"

But her words were cut off when her husband's mouth descended onto hers. His kiss, wild and demanding, was something she could not ignore and did not wish to. So, responding in kind, despite the threat of discovery, it was not long before Avelina wished for more.

Which was precisely when she realized her husband was using both hands to lift her gown. Remembering her surprise, she pulled away and then promptly helped him.

The seamstress had made the fine lace wedding garter as a gift, something Avelina had learned of only when getting dressed. And for which she was grateful. With no mother or family to speak of present, since her brother refused to attend, and without even her own maid, Avelina had been both nervous and a bit shy until donning the very sultry garter and ties.

Knowing her husband would like them, Avelina was proven right as her gown was properly lifted.

Groaning, he knelt in the graveled stone and proceeded to kiss each of her legs around the material. Her hands now in his hair, Avelina relished in the gentle touch, his fingers moving each bit of lace to the side to kiss underneath them as well. By the time he stood, her legs were shaking, Avelina remembering the other times he was between her legs.

He fixed her dress while Avelina used his arms to steady herself to stand. "As dearly as I'd wish to bury myself under your gown," he said, "I fear 'twould be noticeable, the disheveled state of your beautiful wedding finery, when we returned."

"Or," she said, "mayhap you wish to tease and torment me so that I might be shaking for you by the time the evening comes."

Niall cupped her cheeks. "You are already shaking for me, love. And I do enjoy it very much. As I did enjoy my surprise. Though not as much as I will enjoy removing them with my teeth later."

She had no opportunity to explore that visual in her mind before Niall's lips were on hers once again. Avelina would have remained in the garden for the remainder of the day, but the thought of the hall filled with guests, without a bride or groom, had her pulling away.

"We should attend our own wedding feast."

"Mmmm." He did not seem inclined to do so.

Avelina laughed and pulled away further. "Niall." She tugged on his arm, which was like moving a tree trunk. "The guests."

"None of which we know."

"Your brother. Our host?"

At the mention of his brother, Niall's smile faltered. "I am sorry, lass, your brother refused to attend. I'd not have wished you to be wed with no family members present." He frowned. "Even if that family member is your brother."

She reached up to his cheek, wanting to touch him, to thank him for his concern.

Niall closed his eyes when her palm lay there for a moment.

"'Twas my choice to marry so quickly. One I do not regret, family or nay. I've never been one of those maids to dream of my wedding day."

He opened his eyes, and his hand covered hers. "What do you dream of then, my lady wife?"

"You."

Niall smiled. "Before me?"

"Before you, I dreamt of being needed. Marching into battle with my brother and using the skills I've honed to mean something."

He did not laugh at the notion as her brother had.

"From the display I've seen, you'd be quite useful in battle indeed."

"Thank you," Avelina said, having learned, though she was still practicing, to take a compliment without qualifying it. "Shall we go, then?"

Not letting go of her hand but dropping it to their sides, Niall began to walk toward the hall.

"You are my husband," she said, a chill running through Avelina that had naught to do with the crispness of the air.

"And you, my wife."

"Why is that so pleasing to me?"

"That I should call you wife?" he asked as those remaining in the courtyard clapped upon seeing her and Niall. Smiling, Avelina ignored the sudden pang in her chest as she thought of some of her clansmen who would have liked to see her wed.

Of course, not to Niall Duncraig. Which was, of course, the problem.

"Aye," she answered as the front doors of the keep were opened for them.

"For the same reason 'tis pleasing to me," he answered, leaning down to whisper in her ear, "you know what a newly married couple do on their wedding night."

They must have looked very much like the happy couple walking into the great hall, then, Avelina laughing at his words while knowing they were partially true.

As they made their way to the dais, Niall's brother approached them. Standing before her, he looked into her eyes. Something passed between she and the brother, though Avelina could not say precisely what it was. She knew only that looking into his eyes was like looking at one of her own people. A familiarity that should not be there between two strangers, their only interactions thus far with Niall.

"You are family now," he said. "As such..." He knelt, a gesture Avelina did not expect. "I vow to give my life to protect you and will love you like a sister," he said, his head bowed.

Love. The one thing she did not have from her husband, but as she'd told him, it was not an emotion that could be forced. Neither did Avelina need love, as she'd told him, or expect it in a marriage. "Many thanks, my lord."

"Kieran," he said, giving her leave to use his given name.

"Kieran," she amended, the kinship Avelina felt suddenly with her new brother-in-law unexplainable.

"I leave you to your wedding feast." He stepped aside with a brief glance at his brother. Her husband seemed pleased by Kieran's actions. As was she.

Love you like a sister.

Avelina could not be more pleased with her decision. With her husband. Yet that word.

Love.

She'd told Niall she never expected to marry for love, which was true. She did not love him, so surely there was no reason to pine for Niall to feel that way toward her.

What precisely, then, was the fluttering in her stomach when he held her hand as Avelina climbed onto the dais?

Desire. 'Twas desire.

A sensation that did not abate throughout the meal. Sharing a trencher. Niall's fingers grazing hers. By the time their host congratulated them and called for the sweet trays to be brought into the hall, it was well into the day.

"I do believe I may have drunk too much wine," she whispered to her husband.

He peered at her but did not look away. Avelina held her husband's gaze. When he made a sound deep in his throat, her insides twisted and turned. Not in a bad way but turned nonetheless. Her breath caught looking at him. Imagining him between her legs.

"You are a beautiful woman, Avelina."

She was so accustomed to him using Lina that the full use of her name surprised her.

"I do love hearing my name on your lips," she said, oblivious to the revelry around them.

"If you would like, when we share the marriage bed this eve, I will use that name." He leaned into her. "Do you like that, Avelina? Spread your legs wider for me, Avelina, that I might plunge my tongue deeper into you."

He sat back.

"Did you really just say those things at the supper table?"

Niall looked down, as if verifying they were, indeed, sitting at a supper table.

"I believe I did, my love."

She swallowed. "You are a naughty man."

"I am your naughty husband," he responded. "Do not forget it."

"How could I possibly forget such a thing?"

"Mmm."

That seemed to please him.

"A toast," their host called suddenly.

All in the hall raised their mugs and goblets, including the newly married couple.

"Two rivals, seated together, as husband and wife. Let it show all who seek to consider their enemies more than their allies, 'tis better to forge friendships than foster hate. Tannochbrae is proud to host such an event as the union of these two clans."

While everyone toasted to his words, Avelina's stomach did another little dance. This one not as pleasant as the last when her husband gazed at her. 'Twas like a premonition, one that did not settle well with her.

'Tis better to forge friendships than foster hate.

If she'd not met Niall, Avelina would have continued to foster hate toward his clan. Despite their union, she did so for the men who engaged in the Battle of The Black Friars, who killed her father. 'Twas not so easy of a thing to let go of hate.

"Something is amiss," Niall said, watching her.

Avelina shrugged off such thoughts. There would be time later to reconcile her feelings for the clan she'd married into. This was her wedding night, a time not for memories of the past to intrude on the possibilities that lie ahead of them.

"Naught is amiss," Avelina said, but realized she may have spoken too soon.

Her brother appeared at the entrance of the hall just then.

And he was not pleased.

Not pleased at all.

CHAPTER
TWENTY-FOUR

"You are making a spectacle of yourself," Avelina whispered. She and Ewan stood in the corridor, since her brother had refused to enter the hall and had gestured for her to come to him.

Convincing Niall not to accompany her but, instead, to allow her to speak to Ewan alone, had not been easy. But she'd accomplished it and hoped her brother might be reasonable. By his expression, though, that did not seem to be the case.

"I am leaving."

That was not at all what she'd expected.

"Leaving? I do not understand."

They stood to the side of the entrance of the hall, their host and Avelina's husband both watching them.

"I spoke with Tannochbrae just before the feast began. He knows already."

"Leaving. Going home?" she asked, knowing the answer but still not understanding the reasoning for his abrupt departure.

"Aye. There is no reason for me to stay."

"But the cottager? We've still not received word. If he saw something, perhaps—"

"He did not."

Avelina cocked her head to the side. "Oh, did we learn something more? I was not aware—"

"We will learn nothing from him. I'm sure of it."

This was not like her brother at all. He seemed terse, angry almost. Surely this was about the wedding and not the cattle.

"I do wish you'd have attended," she said quietly, changing topics.

Ewan did not flinch. "I would not condone your marriage to a Duncraig."

"Even if I willed it? You are my only close family, Ewan. We've no parents to speak of, no other siblings."

"Because of the man you married," he said, unflinching.

"He. Was. Not. There."

"Regardless." Her brother said no more.

"Why do you leave now? Before nightfall?"

Avelina could not shake the sense something was amiss about his hasty departure.

"I've no wish to remain, to watch you sit beside that man..."

"Ewan." She reached for his hand and was surprised her brother let her take it. "You disagree with my decision, as is your right. But please, do not allow this to come between us."

He squeezed her hand as he may have done when they were children.

"I love you, Sister," he said. "There is naught you could do that would sever the bond we share as siblings."

Avelina's shoulders dropped in relief. "I began to think otherwise."

Her brother squeezed her hand again before dropping it. And then pulled her close. His embrace seemed to signal an end, perhaps, of their lives together as they once were. And though it saddened her, Avelina was always meant to marry, just not, as Ewan had said, a Duncraig clansman.

Nay, not clansman. Chief's son.

"What will you do when you return home?"

"I will continue to make inquiries."

He offered nothing more.

"Make inquiries," she repeated, wondering what that meant precisely. "And if you discover who was behind the attempt at renewing the feud?"

His expression remained passive. "He will be dealt with."

And that was all. Dealt with.

"You do not think my marriage to Niall might begin to heal the wounds of our two clans?"

"I do not."

His tone allowed for no further discussion. And though Avelina did not agree, she could sense there would be no persuading him this eve.

"You will not eat before you leave?"

"I've eaten already and will be on the road while the sun still shines."

At that, she did smile. "It has not shone for days." Her brother looked as if he'd reach out and ruffle her hair as he did when they were young. But likely realizing they were well past the age of hair ruffling, instead he inclined his head.

"Good den, sister. I will send Mary to you with your belongings."

"Only if she is amenable to joining me. If not, please offer her my best wishes and tell her I will come to visit."

Ewan's lips pursed at that. "I cannae tell you that your husband is welcome."

"Ewan," she said, spying that very husband now. He watched them. Had not taken his eyes from them since she'd begun this discussion with her brother.

"I am sorry, Lina. His clan is responsible for—"

She would not hear it. "I know well what his clan is responsible for. There is little need to repeat it."

"Then you know why I cannae welcome him into my hall."

"And when we have children? Will they be welcome into your hall?"

That took him by surprise. "I. . . of course, your children will be welcome."

"They will be Duncraig clansmen, Ewan."

He blinked. Clearly, he had not thought the matter through.

"I. . . we shall deal with that matter when 'tis necessary. I must be on my way," he said, avoiding a topic that would not resolve itself, no matter how much her brother wished it otherwise.

"Go then," she said, knowing there was little else to say. Her stubborn brother would not relent, of that she was certain. "Travel safely, Brother. And do send word if you learn anything more. I am curious who is behind this incident." 'Twas something she'd just considered. "If not for the cattle, I'd not have met Niall."

Her brother winced.

Avelina was unrepentant. Though he cared not for the fact, Niall was her husband now, and Avelina would not rest until Ewan accepted the fact.

"Good den, Lina," he said with a slight bow. "Until we meet again."

"Until we meet again," she said as Ewan left, a pang in her chest reminding Avelina that, despite their differences, she loved her brother deeply. Though it saddened her to part with him, as she looked toward the dais, Lina did not question her decision.

There might not be love between them, but there certainly was an abundance of desire. Even from here Lina could sense it, the expression on Niall's face unmistakable. With every step she took from the hall's entrance toward her husband, the man she'd first met was replaced by a very different look.

One of pleasure.

One of anticipation.

And suddenly, Lina very much wished her wedding feast was over, even if they could not leave before their host. She was ready to get to the wedding night and all that it entailed. And it seemed Niall did, too, because after speaking briefly to the chieftain, Niall stood as if he meant to join her.

They could not leave now.

Could they?

Decorum aside, it seemed precisely like that was what they would do, for Niall's smile as he approached her could only mean one thing.

"Shall we retire, then, my lady wife?"

"Before the host?"

"Aye."

"May we do such a thing?"

He took her hand and tucked it into his elbow, walking back toward where Avelina had just come from. He never answered.

An answer was not necessary.

They were leaving to cheers and some not-so-polite suggestions from the crowd behind them. Ones that once would have made her blush. But now, Avelina simply smiled.

Their wedding night had begun.

CHAPTER
TWENTY-FIVE

H e was going to make this night one Avelina would never forget.

All eve Niall watched her, more pleased by his bride than he ever thought to be since matrimony was not something he enjoyed thinking about. Though his parents had a happy marriage, theirs was not a love match. Not, at least, when they'd wed, though Niall believed his parents had come to love one another.

But 'twas never a marriage of passion, of that he was certain. They were more like friends. Compatible. Happy. The kind of marriage that was common among nobles, but not one Niall particularly looked forward to having.

His own marriage?

Complicated for very different reasons. But that he desired his wife? Of that, there was no doubt. He'd dismissed the maid that attempted to follow them to their chamber, so instead Niall took the girl's duties. As soon as he closed the door behind her, he did not waste a moment.

"Turn around," he demanded.

Lina gave him a brief glance before doing so.

He could not read her look but smiled to himself thinking she likely bristled at the command. His wife was fiercely independent. A bow-wielding maiden who he had no doubt would use her skills if such an occasion warranted it.

But here, in their bedchamber?

"I will remove every piece of fabric from your body," he said, undoing the ties at her back. "Before I lick everything from your neck to your nipples to the very core of you, Lina, I would spin you on the bed, facing down, and continue to lick until you are writhing beneath me. Only when you beg me, when you call out my name so loud that guests remaining in the hall can hear you, will I enter you, giving you all of me. Do you understand?" he asked, spinning her back around.

Eyes wide, Lina watched as he pulled the shoulders of her gown off on each side. Tugging her arms from their sleeves, with her aid, Niall did exactly as he promised. As the gown fell to the floor, he kissed Lina's bare shoulders, the shift she wore blessedly sleeveless.

Bending down, he pulled the gown from under her and stayed close to the floor. Then, one by one, he removed each boot, kissing a trail up under her shift to the wedding garter and straps he'd seen earlier.

"Every bit of clothing," he said, taking it all off piece by piece.

By now Lina was tugging on his plaid, and not wanting her to feel alone in her nakedness, Niall helped his wife remove first the plaid, then linen shirt and boots until they both had nothing to recommend them but their bodies and his promise to her.

"Every bit of you," he promised again, backing Lina up until her legs touched the bed. Lifting her up, he joined Lina on the bed but refused to let her tug him onto her. "A promise is a promise," he said, trying to determine where to start. Spreading her legs apart, Niall decided to begin with the insides of her ankles. And then her calves. He kissed the insides of her knees, and inner thigh all the way up until her fingers threaded through his hair.

"Oh no," he said, as she tried to guide him to her. "Not yet."

Across her stomach and then down her other leg, by the time Niall made his way back up to her breasts, Lina was breathing heavily. Begging him for more.

"Husband," she said, clearly liking the moniker.

Oddly, he did too.

"Mmm," was his only response as he covered her body with his, making his way up her neck toward her mouth. By the time his lips found hers, Lina welcomed him hungrily. Her tongue clashed with his own as Niall's head cocked to the side to give him better access.

Mid-kiss, he reached down between them, pushing her legs open even wider, and guided himself inside. Once fully buried in his wife, Niall began to move. At first, he circled his hips slowly. In and out, he kissed her to the same rhythm of his cock, which was not fully to the hilt inside her.

Reaching between them, he used his thumb to guide her toward release, never breaking the kiss. Her moans against his lips were nearly too much, but he'd not release early. His wife would know pleasure first, and to that end, his thumb moved more quickly. His thrusts became harder and deeper, their pace now almost frantic.

As he thought of her standing beside him at the church, of Lina's uninhibited response to him in the garden, her vulnerability speaking to her brother, the brush of her fingers on their shared trencher...

He broke the kiss to look at her.

"You are mine, Avelina," he said with a possessiveness Niall had never known before. "Mine."

She struggled to catch a breath.

"Say it," he demanded. "You are mine."

"I'm yours," she said. "I am so very yours, Niall. Can you feel it in my response to you?" she asked, circling her hips. Squeezing him to her.

"I can," he said. "Mine," Niall repeated one last time adding, "and I am yours."

At that his wife found release, her nails raking his shoulders, her wetness evident all over his cock. He had no reason to hang on any longer. With a roar of pleasure, he spilled his seed deep within her.

Surely he was no longer among the living.

And yet, some time later, Niall became aware that he was, indeed, lying atop his wife, likely crushing her. Pulling out and falling to her side, he laid there, eyes closed for a moment, wondering what in the goddamn name of the saints had just happened.

He had never been overtaken before with such a possessiveness.

Niall turned his head toward her. Sure enough, Lina was staring at him.

She smiled.

"I am yours," she repeated, confirming she'd not taken offense to his demands.

"Aye," he said. "You are mine." He scooped her into his arms. "I believe I will enjoy having a wife," he said as she tucked her head in his neck.

"And I, a husband."

At that moment, their potential troubles, of which there were many, fell away. All was right, and good. Nothing, it seemed, could come between them. Could break this bond they shared almost from the start.

Niall closed his eyes.

Nothing will come between us.

Nothing.

CHAPTER
TWENTY-SIX

"I wish we could have remained at Tannochbrae," Avelina said not for the first time.

The day after their wedding, when they received word that the cottager had, indeed, seen nothing as her brother predicted, they packed their belongings and rode out. Sleeping under the stars the evening prior, a very different night than their wedding one, along with riding all day, and Avelina really did wish she was arriving at her new home more prepared.

They'd stopped along a river where she had washed dirt from the road off her as best she could. Though Avelina feared 'twould not be her appearance that would come between her and Niall but his family and clan's reaction toward her. The bond between her and her husband continued to grow, but today, Avelina feared, all could change.

"Castle Duncraig," her husband announced as they crested the ridge that until now hid her new home.

"'Tis beautiful," she said. On two sides, the sea, and protection on a third side by a natural inlet. With two courtyards separated by a substantially large keep, both the castle and village off in the distance looked almost as if they were not real. "It would appear the keep is well protected," she said. "Has it ever been successfully attacked?"

"Nay," her brother-in-law replied, obviously proud of the fact.

Avelina thought back to the first conversation she and Niall had about marriage. He'd asked if she truly could live here among those who were, essentially, her enemy.

"You've both accepted me," she said to the two men by her side. Avelina's mount danced under her, likely sensing her worry.

"We have," Kieran said, "and they will too."

"Though mayhap not today," her husband added.

Avelina took a deep breath. Not today, nor tomorrow. But they would. Both Niall and Kieran had, and Avelina had come to accept them as well.

They did not kill your father.

She did not know who struck that blow, but there would be men, including the chief, who had been in that battle.

"Lina?" her husband called her name as if it were not the first time.

"I am ready," she said, though in truth, she was not at all. But at her words, Niall spurred his mount forward as the three of them descended the hill.

It was not until they were well past the gatehouse and into the inner courtyard that the whispers began. None would know she was a MacKinlay, but her arrival with Niall and Kieran was enough, apparently, to set tongues wagging. And wag they did. By the time they'd dismounted, a crowd had gathered around them. Most openly stared at her, but none asked the silent question Niall did not seem to be willing to answer. Instead, he helped Avelina dismount, whispered, "Come with me," to her, and took her by the hand.

"My saddlebags," she said, "and bow."

"Kieran will see they are taken care of."

Kieran winked at her as Niall led Avelina toward the keep.

"There are four floors," he said as they approached. "The stores and soldiers' quarters below." He indicated the ground floor as the two of them made their way to a set of stone stairs built into the side of the keep. "This forebuilding," he said of the section they were about to enter, "was added when I was a boy."

"The extra defense seems unnecessary," she said. "Castle Duncraig is well-fortified by water on three sides."

"But 'tis the fourth side that matters most," he said.

The guard at the door greeted them. Niall nodded as his man opened the large wooden door.

They walked into a room that separated the forebuilding from the remainder of the keep. Passing through it and another door, the unmistakable sounds of a great hall reached her ears.

"And as you can see, on this floor, the hall."

They passed through a corridor lit by wall torches and through yet another doorway, though this one remained open. It was well past supper, she assumed, but still the hall was not empty. There were servants wiping tables and at least five or six others milling about, two playing chess, and the others seeming to drink ale and do naught else.

Niall pointed to one of the men who stood beside a table. Though the man spoke with those sitting, he did not appear to be drinking with them. "Finlay is our steward. Actually, he's the son of a blacksmith, but my father, as a teen, noticed his natural intelligence and how hard he worked. The two struck up a friendship, Finlay eventually becoming our steward not long after my father became chief."

"My lord," Finlay said, as if sensing Niall despite having his back to him. "You've just returned," he said, approaching. The man was probably the same age as her father would have been.

Master Finlay looked between them. He didn't have to wait long.

"Finlay, I would like you to meet my wife, Lady Avelina. Perhaps you can tell me where I might find my parents to apprise them that I've returned. With a wife."

Avelina could not help but smile at the steward's surprised expression.

"I am pleased to make your acquaintance, Master Finlay."

He bowed, "And yours, my lady."

Avelina noticed her husband failed to mention her surname.

"I believe both of your parents returned to the solar chamber after supper, my lord. Shall I have meals sent there for you?"

"Nay," Niall replied. "We will go to them and then to my chambers. If you would have a bath and meal sent there."

"Of course, my lord."

Leaving the befuddled steward, Niall led Avelina from the hall up another set of stone stairs. "In this, the great tower, are my parents' chambers and their solar. I am in the east tower, which is where we will remain for now."

"For now?"

We'd not talked about our living arrangements beyond returning.

"I've a property within a half day's ride I had intended to reside in once married. We can visit it on the morrow if you would like. I must speak to my father about the arrangement."

"Should you not remain here, as his second-in-command?"

"We discussed it, but the manor is close enough. But we shall speak to him."

Much too soon, they stood outside a door where Niall's parents were currently located. He must have sensed her worry, because Niall took her hand.

"Lina?"

She looked into his eyes.

"'Twill be well, love," he said.

Though he'd used the term before, this time Niall said it in a way that made her believe just possibly...

The moment was gone. He knocked at the door and waited.

A man who looked nearly identical to her husband, albeit with some gray hair and more lines in his face than Niall, opened the door. She'd not meant to squeeze Niall's hand looking upon his father, but every part of her tensed as she tried to push aside the feeling. Openly hating the man would do little to endear either of his parents to her.

He looked back and forth between them before opening the door wider.

"'Tis Niall," a woman said. Though how his mother knew her son had returned without being able to see him, Avelina was unsure.

Her father-in-law shook her husband's hand and then stood aside.

"Our son, aye, and..."

He watched her carefully as Lina followed Niall into the

chamber. He still held her hand, which seemed to be the first thing his mother noticed.

Avelina had not been expecting her to look so young. Or to have red hair as there was not a trace of the color in Niall's. She appeared younger than her husband and quite beautiful, in fact. A handsome couple to be certain.

"And my wife," he promptly announced, releasing her hand and stepping toward his mother. Leaning down, he kissed her on the forehead. A gesture he'd done many times by the casual nature of it.

Returning to Avelina, he held her hand once more, for which she was grateful.

Of course, his parents could not have appeared more surprised.

"Your wife?" His mother seemed less pleased than his father.

"Lady Avelina," Niall said. "I would introduce you to my parents. Kenneth, the chief of Clan Duncraig, and my mother, Lady Mairi."

"Pleased to meet you both," she ground out, wishing to mean the words. Alas, she did not. Could not. Unlike her husband, the chief fought in that battle. Had killed members of her clan. Perhaps her family.

Maybe even her father.

But for Niall's sake...

Something made her want to tell them. Not to hide it a moment longer. "Avelina MacKinlay," she added. "Sister to the chief of Clan MacKinlay."

A chill ran through her at his parents' expressions. His mother appeared to be in disbelief. His father?

Clearly angry.

"You married Chief MacKinlay's sister?" he asked Niall.

At the same time, his mother stood. "Son. What have you done?"

Niall gripped her hand even tighter.

His father said, "This marriage will not stand. The chief's son will not take a MacKinlay wife," he said, as if Avelina was not standing beside him.

"It will, Father. We've consummated the marriage."

Consummated it before the wedding day, in fact. But there seemed no need to mention that to his parents.

"My child," his mother said, coming toward her. "This must be difficult for you, dear?"

Though his mother initially seemed the more upset of the two, her expression now was one of empathy.

Avelina found her voice. "I will admit 'tis somewhat difficult, aye."

She peeked at the chief.

He glared at her.

Avelina's chin raised in defiance.

"Why?" the chief asked again. Though he looked at her, the question was clearly for Niall.

"An affinity grew between us. And I would not dishonor her by taking the lady's maidenhood without making her my wife."

Her cheeks warmed. Though they'd discussed telling his parents that particular fact, knowing 'twas likely necessary, Avelina had still hoped it could be avoided.

"If you wanted to bed a woman, surely you could have found one who was not a MacKinlay."

"Kenneth," his mother scolded.

But the first salvo had been shot.

"Surely I did not intend to wed a man whose family slaughtered my own," she said.

"Oh dear," his mother said. But Avelina's attention was on the father.

"But you did. Why?"

She would not back down. "As Niall said, an affinity grew between us as we traveled together to learn the source of the cattle's movement from our land to yours."

He addressed Niall. "And did you learn of it?"

"Nay," Niall said. "Avelina's brother continues to investigate the matter. They've been returned, but we do not yet know by who, or why it happened."

That clearly did not please his father.

"Someone attempted to renew the feud."

"And we," Avelina added, "are attempting to mollify it."

Her meaning, clear.

"Perhaps this union is, indeed, a good thing," his mother said. "Kenneth, think on it. We do not wish to renew the feud, and their marriage may even bring our two clans together."

His father addressed Niall, finally turning away from Avelina who was grateful for the respite.

"We will never be allies with Clan MacKinlay."

It was as if he'd struck her in the chest.

"Kenneth," his mother repeated. Then she said to Niall, "Perhaps you should take Lady Avelina for a respite after your travels."

"Perhaps I should take her to Glenhaven this eve rather than on the morrow."

"You will retire to Glenhaven without speaking with me first?" his father asked, his voice hard.

"I am finding it difficult to speak with you at all," Niall said.

"You would not reach it before nightfall and have

already been traveling," his mother said. Stay, Niall, and we will speak again in the morn."

Her tone was almost pleading, and clearly it was one Niall could not deny.

"As you wish, Mother," he said. "Come," her husband said to her.

He did not address his father before tugging on her hand and leading Avelina toward the door. Neither did she wish to speak with the chief any further, though she would thank his mother for her courtesy.

"I am very pleased to meet you," she said, this time with the warmth that her first greeting had lacked. "And thank you for your hospitality."

"'Tis more than hospitality, my dear. You are my daughter-in-law. You are family. And this is your home."

Her words could not have been a more straightforward show of support. So very different than the chief who said nothing amidst their exchange.

"I am grateful for it," Avelina said, appreciative of her support.

They left the solar without any other words spoken. And it was not until they'd reached the end of the corridor and climbed another set of stairs that Niall pulled Avelina into his arms. Wordlessly, he kissed her. Slowly. Deeply.

And if she did not know otherwise, Avelina might have even thought of it as lovingly.

CHAPTER
TWENTY-SEVEN

Niall stood by the bed for a long time, watching as his wife slept.

He should have gone already. Wanted to be back before she woke. But Niall just could not pull himself away from the sight. 'Twas still dark, but the candlelight provided enough light to illuminate her face.

In the light, while she was awake, she would be more cautious as if she were attempting to prove herself, something Niall was certain Avelina had done for a long time. Wanting to prove her worth against threats which, to be fair, were plentiful for her. A woman who'd lost nearly everything.

Her father.

Her mother.

Her relatives and clansmen.

And now, her brother.

But she'd gained a husband, one who would not allow her to continue to suffer. Which is why he did finally tear himself from her bedside to seek out his own father. As Niall suspected, he was already in the hall, well before the servants served the morning meal. He sat as he always did, before the fire, a chess board in front of him. Though he'd have more privacy in his solar, Niall's father had always said if he would use the early morning hours to think, then he'd do so where his people knew where to find him.

And they did.

Even before the sun rose, 'twas not unusual to find a servant or other retainer or one of Duncraig's warriors sitting beside his father asking a question or for advice. And when they were not, the chief would simply stare at the chess board thinking. Considering. Waiting.

Niall sat across from him.

Saying nothing, he leaned forward and began to play. His father watched Niall's move and made one of his own.

"You were unkind to her," Niall began, knowing this discussion would not be an easy one.

"She is not just any woman, Son. You brought a MacKinlay—*the* MacKinlay."

"I did, indeed. And would not have done so lightly. Surely you must realize that."

His father frowned. "Your mother said the same. But that matters little. Fact is, she's the enemy. Always has been. Always will be. Your clansmen will not take kindly to her."

"My clansmen or you? I and Kieran have taken kindly to her as does, it seems, Mother, even after I deprived her of my wedding ceremony."

"A fact she finds difficult to reconcile," his father said, waiting for his move.

"As expected."

"I do not agree with the union, but why could you not have brought her here to wed? For your mother?"

"Her brother would not have easily allowed such a thing. And as you said, you do not agree with the union."

"You knew I would not."

"Aye."

"But married the lass anyway."

"Aye."

"Yet not for love?"

Did he love her?

Niall would have said nay just days ago, but he'd be a fool to deny the feelings he had toward his wife were unlike any he'd had for a woman before.

He cared for her.

Wished to be with her always.

Wanted to protect her.

Make love to her all day and night.

Did he love her? How was one to know?

"Son," his father said as Niall hesitated. "You could have made alliances with your marriage."

"Perhaps I am."

His father laughed bitterly. "With Clan MacKinlay? Never."

As they continued to play, Niall losing the advantage, he found himself curious as to the reason. "It seems if anyone would be resistant to an alliance, it would be MacKinlays. It was their clan, after all, that was nearly decimated."

His words were not endearing him to his father.

"Clan MacKinlay was ordered to that battle as we were. We lost men that day as well. You do not remember what led to it, Son, as you were too young."

"Though I know the tales. It seems both clans were equally to blame for the feud."

His father scowled and made a move Niall was unlikely

to overcome. "You know nothing of what you speak. Clan MacKinlay will never be our allies," he repeated.

"Yet those who remain, like Avelina and her brother, were not at that battle. Nor took part in any of the activities that led to it. A generation has passed—"

"Four generations will pass before I welcome a MacKinlay into my hall."

"Including my wife? Our children?"

Another move. Niall had lost. Too quickly.

But he would not lose the most important fight.

"What did the chief of Clan MacKinlay say about his sister marrying you?"

As always, his father refused to give him an answer. He treated Niall as if he were a child at times. Including now.

"He was not pleased."

"Where did you marry?"

"At Tannochbrae. We were there questioning the reposting of the cattle."

"On Tannochbrae land."

"Aye."

"Did the brother attend the ceremony?"

"Nay," Niall admitted.

"Then, for once, MacKinlay and I are in agreement."

"Nor did her brother attend the wedding feast the chieftain hosted. Tannochbrae was exceedingly gracious."

"And will be rewarded for it, even if I do not agree with the union."

"So that is your answer then? You will not accept Avelina here? Shall I go to Glenhaven then? Perhaps you wish to name another as your second?"

HIs heart thudded in his chest. Niall was sorry it had come to this, but he would not have Avelina be mistreated.

"I would think on the matter," his father said.

It was not the answer he'd hoped for.

Never in his life had Niall disagreed with his father on such an important matter. It seemed he'd been too generous in his mind about his father's ability to forgive. Something he'd do well to learn from Avelina.

Niall stood. "Very well. I will not have Avelina hurt, believing she is not wanted here. We go to Glenhaven immediately. I will await your decision, Father."

If he thought his father would soften his stance, Niall was to be disappointed. He dealt less with the man who'd given him life than the chief of Duncraig now. His father's nose flared, but he gave no other indication he'd heard him.

Turning on his heel, he retreated from the hall. He would speak with his mother and then take Avelina from here. From his home.

The only one he'd ever known.

Take her away. . . perhaps, forever.

CHAPTER
TWENTY-EIGHT

"Thank you for the gowns, my lady," Avelina said as her mother-in-law came into the chamber.

When she'd woken up to find Niall gone, Avelina began to dress herself. Missing Mary, not only for the aid she provided but for her companionship as well, she'd been about to slip on the one gown that did not tie in the back when a knock at the door interrupted her.

A serving maid entered, her arms laden with new gowns.

They'd chosen one, and Avelina dressed wondering where Niall had gone. To speak with his father? He'd mentioned doing so last eve.

Heat crept up her shoulders to her cheeks thinking of their wedding night. How many times they made love. What her husband had done to her. How could Avelina not know 'twas possible? She would speak with Mary on the matter, the only married woman she knew who could have and should have mentioned such things.

Another knock sounded, and this time, 'twas Niall's mother.

"You are most welcome," Mairi said, closing the bedchamber door behind her. Sitting in a high-backed wooden chair, she watched as the maid placed braids on each side of Avelina's hair, pulling them back and tying the pieces together.

"I am sorry for the welcome you received," his mother said. "'Twas quite a surprise to learn Niall had married."

"And married to a MacKinlay," Avelina added.

"Aye."

The maid did not flinch. Likely by now, word had spread, and all of Castle Duncraig knew of Niall's new bride.

"I do not harbor as much hate and resentment as my husband. Or as you must for our clan," the lady ventured.

On this, Avelina was torn. "I've hated for so long," she said. "And did not expect to feel anything but for the rest of my days. Until I met your son."

"He is an extraordinary man."

"Indeed, he is," Avelina agreed.

The maid finished. Avelina's mother-in-law nodded to her as if in dismissal. With a quick bob, she did then leave.

"And I imagine you are an extraordinary woman to have captured his attention. Niall has not shown any proclivity to marry until now."

"I cannae tell you I've wanted to marry either, despite my brother's urging."

"Until Niall?"

"Aye."

"My son, for many reasons, has never been a spontaneous one. He carefully plans, to a fault, and so you can understand our surprise in this."

Avelina sat on the edge of the bed.

"The healer," she said. "He leaves nothing to chance because of it. Because of his guilt."

His mother's facial expression showed her surprise. "He told you of it?"

"Aye."

She blinked. "Niall never speaks of the matter."

"He was but a boy, my lady." Avelina found herself defending him, forgetting for a moment this was the one woman she'd never have to do such a thing with. She was his mother. And suddenly, Avelina was filled with a warmth for her, a gratitude. . . no matter she was supposed to be the enemy.

This woman was no more an enemy to her than Niall.

"If you will, please call me Mairi," she said.

"And me, Lina." Avelina smiled. Her mother-in-law did the same.

The door opened.

Avelina's heart raced with every step Niall took toward her. But as she saw his expression, her smile faded.

"Niall?"

He strode to his mother, kissed her on the forehead, and joined Avelina on the edge of the bed. Taking one of her hands in his, Niall raised it, kissed it, and folded it into both of his own on his lap.

How had she lived without this man until now?

"We are leaving," he announced. "For Glenhaven."

So, the talk with his father had not gone well.

"When?" his mother asked.

"At once."

Avelina's shoulders sank.

"Surely you will break your fast first?"

Niall shook his head. "Cook has prepared warm bread for us to take on the road. Our mounts," he said to Avelina, "are being prepared. Once we gather our belongings, we will be off."

"Tell me," Mairi said. "What did he say?"

Niall's jaw clenched. "That he will think on the matter."

"The matter being me?" Avelina offered. "If he will accept me into your family?"

The look Niall gave her was one of sorrow and of pity. And though Avelina should be angry, for it was his father she needed to forgive for his role in the battle, it was neither anger or hate that consumed her.

But sorrow. For Niall.

"When my brother refused to attend the wedding ceremony," Avelina said, "I wanted to rail at him for his stubbornness. But I realized that, even though I had—" Avelina nearly said, 'had fallen in love with you,' to Niall. Where had that come from? "Even though affection had grown between Niall and me, that did not mean the same had happened for my brother. But perhaps, I hoped, it would in time. Once he realizes the alternative is losing a sister...and someday, nieces or nephews."

"Kieran accepted us easily enough." Niall looked toward his mother. "As have you, Mother."

Mairi sighed. "Some have more capacity than others for forgiveness," she said. "Based on their own experiences. Your father," she looked at Avelina, "your brother. I believe will come to our side eventually."

"I believe the same," Avelina said, though her words were more confident than she truly felt.

"And if he does not?" Niall asked his mother. "I will not serve as Duncraig's second if Father does not accept Avelina fully into our clan."

The words she least wanted to hear. And yet, she and Niall had spoken of the possibility. He'd asked her once if she could truly leave her home and make one here with Clan Duncraig. She'd been less certain then than she was now, that aye, she could do so for him. For Niall.

But now, 'twas Niall's turn to answer the question.

"Would you have married me knowing it might lead to this?"

Was it a fair question to ask? Especially in front of his mother? Avelina was not sure, but neither could she stop herself from voicing the question aloud.

Niall looked between her and his mother. At first, Avelina thought he would not answer the question.

But he did. "I cannae know what I'd have done but can say only it matters not. We are married, and I will protect you from anyone who wishes you harm. Today and always."

It was not the answer she'd hoped for, but Avelina was grateful for the last portion of his words. As he and his mother spoke of their leave-taking and of his father, Avelina remained quiet. Thinking of her question. And of his answer.

I cannae know what I'd have done.

And that's when she realized, Avelina had fallen in love with her husband. And wished for him to have done the same. To have said, "Aye. For love, I'd have done anything." But of course, he did not say those words. Niall had affection for her, not love. He's said as much many times.

But something had shifted between them. Her previous words now rang hollow.

"Come, lady wife." Niall stood and urged her to do the same. "I will take you to our new home."

Words that could have, should have, been joyful. And yet, they were anything but.

CHAPTER
TWENTY-NINE

They arrived well before dark.

Glenhaven Manor had been given to Niall when he was born, the estate having belonged in his family for many years. Though a manor house, it was lightly fortified with an outer wall on two sides that did not face the sea and a gatehouse that had recently been rebuilt.

"This is Glenhaven?"

Lina rode beside him, clearly pleased.

"It is not as grand as some, your home and mine included."

"But it is perfect," she said. "The view." She breathed in the salt air. Though they'd ridden mostly along the coast, here they could actually spy the sea in the distance due to the landscape.

"There is a small village there," he pointed north, "over that ridge. We've all we need here," he said, "but—"

Niall stopped.

Then he spurred his mount forward and Lina followed.

He'd been about to say, "but many retreat south to Castle Duncraig and its village and on market days when they need supplies not found here." Would they do so if his father did not accept Lina?

Likely not.

The possibility of such a state was something he'd considered the entire way to Glenhaven. Along with his wife's question.

Would he have married her?

Knowing she may not have been accepted by his father? Knowing he may be forced to renounce his claim to become the next chief of Duncraig? 'Twas all he'd ever known. All he'd trained for. And yet, he looked at Lina now, watched her as she took in what was to be her new home.

Aye, he'd have married her. And should have told her so. *What held me back?*

She may very likely not be married to the next chief of Duncraig but, instead, to a man with no purpose. For so long, he'd avoided making rash decisions, knowing the potential consequences. But then he'd gone and made the rashest one of all.

Marrying a MacKinlay.

Nay, he did not regret it. But she may.

"They realize 'tis you," she said as they approached the gatehouse that was opened for them well before he and Lina reached it. As she'd said, word seemed to have spread, and not only were the gates open, but by the time they rode through into the courtyard, a small crowd had gathered. There were just enough servants here to maintain the manor and enough warriors to defend it.

"My lord," the steward of Glenhaven, a man who had served his clan since well before Niall had been born, greeted them.

Niall dismounted and prepared to introduce his wife and steward to each other.

"This is Angus," Niall said, not wishing to let go of his wife's waist but knowing he must for now. "A loyal and trusted member of Clan Duncraig and steward of Glenhaven Manor. Do not allow his gruffness to hide his kind heart. None care more deeply for the people here than Angus." He did not care the steward now gave him a look of reproach for admitting such a thing to Lina.

Niall relied on that kind heart now. None had a reputation quite like Angus here at Glenhaven, and his opinion of Lina would be important.

"Angus," he said, aware they now had an audience. "I am pleased to introduce you to my wife, Lady Avelina MacKinlay, sister to the chief of Clan MacKinlay."

Angus blinked.

Gasps and whispers told Niall all had heard his words. He would have them know immediately and also understand she was his bride by choice.

"I have a great affection for the woman by my side, now the lady of Glenhaven, and know you will too."

Angus bowed. "I am certain of it," he said finally. Standing, he addressed Lina. "Welcome, my lady, to Glenhaven. I would be pleased to offer you a tour if my lord wills it?"

Niall would very much like to give his wife a tour himself, but having her be in Angus's company would serve them more.

"My lady?" Niall asked her.

"I would very much enjoy that," she said.

"Very well." Angus offered her his arm. "We will see to your belongings. My lord, the evening meal is being prepared. I shall escort your wife there upon the conclusion of our tour. Unless of course," he said to Lina, "you would prefer to be taken to your chamber first?"

"Just briefly," she said, "so that I may change my gown."

"Of course. You travel with no lady's maid?"

"I do not," Lina said. "Though I do hope my maid will be joining me here soon."

"You remain at Glenhaven for. . ." Angus trailed off.

"Permanently," Niall added. Even if his father did welcome them in his hall, it would be here they would reside.

Angus's smile at that could not be contrived. He seemed truly glad to hear the news.

"Very good, my lord." And then he asked Lina, "Shall we?"

Before Niall could even properly bid his wife adieu, Angus had whisked her off. Lina was now greeting well-wishers who seemed alternatively cautious and, some of them, pleased. He had no doubt it did matter that she was a MacKinlay. But just then, it seemed to matter less than he expected, and much less than his father or Lina's brother would have them believe.

Smiling at the thought, Niall grabbed the reins of his horse intending to stable him himself. Perhaps all would be well here, and Lina would be welcomed the way she deserved.

"A MacKinlay," someone muttered behind him.

When Niall turned to uncover the culprit, none gave themselves away.

He could question them and discover who said it. Instead, Niall walked away.

Or perhaps, her welcome would not be what he'd hoped for.

～

"I would speak to you, my lord."

The day had gone better than expected. Aside from the one comment when they'd arrived, Niall had heard no other unkind remarks about his wife, and during the evening meal, he'd spied nothing out of the ordinary.

It seemed as though Lina, as a MacKinlay, did not matter to his people here, but Niall also knew most would not dare anger him by being openly hostile.

Unlike his father.

"Of course," he said, watching Lina leave the hall with the lady's maid Angus had found for her. "I would speak to you as well."

Moving to an alcove just outside the hall for privacy, Niall did not hesitate. "Tell me all."

Angus shook his head. "I was surprised, of course. Had heard of the incident with the cattle and assumed you had gone to MacKinlay about the matter. Why else would you have been in the presence of the chief's sister?"

"Why indeed," he agreed.

"A wife. And a MacKinlay wife," the old man mused. "Your father did not take the news well?"

Before coming to Glenhaven, Angus had served with Niall's father for many years and knew him well.

"Nay, he did not. Refuses to accept his daughter-in-law."

Angus did not seem surprised.

"So you are here."

"Aye," Niall said. "Though we'd planned to reside here, I did not think 'twould be necessary to give up my position as the chief's second."

That did seem to surprise Angus. "Did he say as much?"

"If he will not accept her. . ." There was naught else to say on the matter.

"I see why you fell in love with the woman, despite her clan's affiliation."

"I am not—"

Angus laughed. "You may not know love, son, but this old man knows the affliction well."

Angus had been married for many years. When his wife fell ill and died, he remarried. But when he lost his second wife, Angus vowed never to do so again. And had not.

"I care deeply for her and married Lina so not to be parted from her."

"It is no weakness to admit to love."

Niall wished to steer the path in another direction. "How was your tour?"

"We got along, if that's what you wish to know. I will admit my initial thoughts had not been kind. 'Tis been many years since I've been in the presence of a MacKinlay. But Lady Avelina..."

"Did you tell her you fought in the Battle of The Black Friars?"

"I did," he said. "Told the lady most sincerely I was sorry for the loss she bore because of it. But also stated I knew her father to be an honorable man, even as he was considered an enemy."

"Men can be both, I suppose."

"And women too."

"What did Lina reply?"

"That together we would learn to bury the past and forge a new future."

The corners of Niall's lips raised. "Do you believe such a thing is possible?"

"Mmm. I would not have believed I'd spend the afternoon giving a tour to the new lady of Glenhaven, the chief of MacKinlay's sister."

Angus liked her, and Niall was pleased by the fact.

He liked her too.

Nay. He loved her.

And would tell her so.

"I am glad you can see beyond her surname, Angus," he said, unused to sharing such things with the stalwart steward.

"He will come around to her," Angus said without acknowledging Niall's words.

"And if he does not?"

Both men remained silent. The implications of such a thing were too great to contemplate. Neither would the problem be solved that eve. Another, his absence from Lina, could be more easily overcome.

Niall clasped Angus on the shoulder. "You are a good man, and I am grateful for your service here. And your treatment of my wife."

"No thanks are necessary," the old man said. "Now go to her. Glenhaven may be her home now, but the manor is foreign to her."

"A fine suggestion," Niall replied.

He intended to do just that. And would have, if his friend and steward had not reached one hand to Niall's shoulder to steady himself, grasping his chest with the other one.

Beads of sweat formed on Angus's head as he suddenly struggled to breathe.

His beloved steward, friend, clansman, was going to die.

CHAPTER
THIRTY

"Pheasant pie?" Avelina asked as she walked into the kitchens.

"Aye," said Cook, a woman twice Avelina's age who had been as kind to her as everyone else here at Glenhaven. "I was told we would double the number in our hall by eve?"

It had been three days since Angus had fallen ill. Thankfully, today was the day Duncraig's healer would arrive along with a "party" that none knew who it included. Niall had immediately sent a message of Angus's condition, that he did not appear to be improving, when the messenger returned last eve saying "all were on their way to Glenhaven."

All.

Did that mean his parents too?

Niall believed so as they both held a special fondness for a man they considered to be family. Suddenly, her reception at Glenhaven meant little compared to the question all had been asking for days.

Would Angus survive?"

Niall admitted he thought the steward was going to die in front of him that night they'd arrived, and Lina had little to say to comfort him knowing the incident was most upsetting. She'd held him, made love to him, and done all she could to ensure theirs was an easy transition coming into the role of lord and lady of Glenhaven. The healer, apparently not as skilled as Duncraig's, said there was naught to do but accompany him while Angus sometimes lay peacefully and at other times seemed to be in pain. He spoke little, but his eyes said all.

Despite herself, Avelina found she'd developed a kinship with the man who would make his passing as difficult to bear as if she'd known him for many years. Unexplainable, aye, but a fact nonetheless.

"I was told the same," she told Cook, "and am here to ask if you need anything at all."

"Nay, my lady," Cook said. "Many thanks for asking."

"They've arrived," a young serving boy called from the entrance of the kitchen. "They are here."

Avelina picked up the hem of her gown, one Mairi had given her, and hurried up the stone stairs of the kitchens to the courtyard above. As the boy had said, a riding party had just arrived. And it included the one person Avelina did not wish to see so soon.

He looked directly at her. Avelina, never one to look away, raised her chin and walked toward the group. She curtsied along with the others as a sign of respect for the chief, even if Avelina wished to do anything but. Thus far, the people here had been kind to her, and she'd not give them any reason to do otherwise. A slight to their chief would not do well.

It seemed all from Duncraig had come. Niall's parents, his brother, so many she did not know. Including a woman her husband watched so carefully, wearily, that it could only be...

The healer.

She'd been pulled in a wagon, but the moment the older woman stepped down to the ground, her cane aiding her, Avelina's suspicions were confirmed.

Going to her husband, Avelina took his hand as he greeted the healer. She assumed the healer would treat Niall coldly, knowing her husband still bore much guilt from the incident, so Avelina was surprised she did anything but.

"You look well," she said, "a wife becomes you."

Niall introduced her to the healer just as his mother joined them.

"Son," she said, as Niall leaned toward his mother and kissed her on the cheek. "Lady Avelina." Her mother-in-law did the same to her. "You both do, indeed, look well. Glenhaven agrees with you," she said to Lina.

"Very much, my lady," she said. Then to the healer she said, "We shall take you to Angus at once."

So it was that Lina found herself in Angus's bedchamber with the healer, her husband, and his parents and brother.

"There are too many," the healer said. "Leave us."

Lina made to do as she was bid until the healer stopped her. "Lady Mairi. Lady Avelina. If you would remain."

Mairi chuckled.

So, she wanted the men to leave? Avelina returned to Angus's bedside, taking the man's hand in her own. As she did so, she looked up just as the chief turned back to her. It seemed he noticed she held Angus's hand. Niall's father stopped in the doorframe and raised his head, his eyes locking with her own.

It was as if he was seeing her for the first time. The chief's brows furrowed, the man confused about something, though Avelina could not say what precisely. And then, he left.

"Tell me all," Mairi said as the door was closed, and so Avelina did. Of what Niall described to her. Of Angus's pain when he woke. Of how often he slept and the worries they had that, one day, he would not wake again.

The healer placed her hand on his chest. At that, Angus woke. He seemed to recognize the healer and Mairi, but instead of saying anything to them, he groaned and closed his eyes once more.

"Angus is ill in his breast. Death has penetrated him and taken up its abode."

Avelina knew not what the woman meant, but she did not care for her words.

"Lady Avelina," the healer said directly to her. "I will need a tehua berry, poppy plant, peppermint, and red sexet seeds."

Aveliana did not recognize all of what she'd asked for, but she knew who might be able to give her aid. Releasing Angus's hand, she stood.

"Of course," she said. "At once."

Just as Avelina was about to open the chamber door, a hand on her shoulder stopped her.

"You care for him," her mother-in-law said.

"Aye," she said. "Angus had been most kind to me for the few days he was. . ." She could not say it. "He cannae die," she said.

"Go, get the herbs she asks for. Do not fret for Angus. She is quite skilled," Mairi said. And then she added, "I am glad for it. That you've found a home here."

"None have been unkind to me," she said. "If they are displeased, they do not tell me or my husband."

Mairi smiled. "I am glad for it," she repeated as Avelina opened the door then, wishing to retrieve the herbs the healer asked for as quickly as possible. It was only as she closed the wooden door that Avelina realized she was not alone.

The chief of Clan Duncraig stood watch just outside the bedchamber door. And was alone.

She. And the chief.

CHAPTER
THIRTY-ONE

"Where is Father?" Kieran asked.

Niall looked around the hall but did not see him. "Did he not come from Angus's chamber behind us?"

Kieran shrugged as they sat before the hearth that now roared with a fire to keep out the chill. Even in summer months, when Glenhaven would be at its warmest, the fire roared. As servants began to prepare for supper around them, Niall and Kieran spoke of Angus. Of Duncraig. And eventually, of their father.

"Has he spoken of it?" Niall asked his brother.

"Nay." Kieran shook his head. "The stubborn old goat refuses to, though I've tried more than once. How has she been received here?"

"Better than expected." A pang in his chest made Niall envision the frail man in his bed abovestairs who had collapsed in his arms. "Angus," he said. No other words were necessary. The bond between his wife and the steward , though briefly formed, was evident for all to see in his chamber.

"Angus." Kieran accepted a mug from a serving woman who poured his ale and then she did the same with Niall. "He will not survive, will he?"

Niall simply did not know. "The healer—"

"Apologize to her."

He would have, should have, many years ago. "I cannae."

"Aye, brother, you can. She will forgive you, and you will be better for it."

The two fell silent as the hall came alive between them. They spoke of other things, of the MacKinlay cattle, all but the most important matter. What would happen if Niall's father did not accept his wife? If he was forced to give up his place in the clan?

"Kieran. If I am not second, there is no man better suited for the position than you. I would be proud to serve you," he said, meaning the words.

"Nay," his brother immediately dismissed him. "I will not allow such talk."

"In many ways, you are more well suited to it."

"Niall," his brother said again. "Nay."

The more he thought on the matter, the more Niall realized his words rang true. Kieran would make a fine chief. Would any reject him for not being his father's natural-born son? Niall was unsure of the answer to that question, but of his leadership abilities, he was more certain.

They both stood as the chief of Clan Duncraig approached them.

As always, his father appeared ready for battle, even if 'twas just with words. Niall raised his arm for a serving girl as his father joined them, and all three sat once again.

"I would speak with you on the matter of your wife," his father said without preamble, as was his custom.

Niall, prepared to defend her, leaned forward. Niall watched his father and, knowing him well, realized he had come to a decision. His fate would be decided in this very moment.

But unlike the day he'd arrived at Glenhaven, he was not filled with despair at the thought of losing his place in the clan. He'd gained much, much more.

"Angus accepted her," he said. 'Twas a statement, and not a question.

"He did," Niall said.

"He is more of a man than I have been."

Niall and Kieran exchanged a glance. Had he heard his father correctly?

Surely not.

Though they were separated from others in the hall, it also seemed a very public place to have such a discussion. Especially if his father truly meant those words.

"You may have to repeat yourself," Kieran said, echoing Niall's thoughts.

"I spent many years hating Clan MacKinlay. When you brought Lady Avelina home as your wife, I allowed that hate to overtake the love I bear you," he said to Niall. "I am sorry for it, Son."

His father had rarely spoken of his love for either him or Kieran, even if they knew it was there. And he apologized, especially to his sons, even less than that.

Niall had no words to offer.

Kieran, it seemed, had none either.

"If I wish to find quiet in my hall," his father said finally, "I know how to achieve it."

"You will admit, Father," Niall said, "your words are uncommon for you."

"A man admits when he is wrong."

"You decided this abovestairs with Angus?" Kieran seemed to have finally found his voice as well.

Their father may apologize, but he did not seem inclined to further explain himself.

He did say to Niall, "I've thought of nothing else since you left, as I told you I would."

Though he was grateful, Niall also needed his father to understand what his words truly meant. "It is my wife you should offer your apology to, not I," he said.

"As I've done."

Another surprise.

"I spoke with her outside Angus's chamber. Lady Avelina is as gracious as your mother claims. She accepted it, and I welcomed her to our clan."

"Where is she now?" Niall asked.

"Gathering herbs or finding someone to gather them for her, I suppose, for the healer."

The healer.

A man admits when he is wrong.

He stood. Niall should have done this many, many years ago.

"I am glad for this, Father," he said. "Although I will say that I reconciled my brother as second in my stead. He would do as well or better than I in the role." Both his father and Kieran looked as if they would argue with him, but Niall would not be waylaid. "Now, if you will pardon me, I must speak to someone at once."

And that someone happened to be sitting in Angus's bedchamber along with his mother. But this could not wait.

"Will you allow us," he asked his mother, "a moment alone?"

His mother smiled and wordlessly inclined her head, leaving the chamber.

The healer sat with her hands on her lap beside Angus's bed. He seemed to be sleeping, though, thankfully, and not in any pain.

"It was I who chased you that night," he said without preamble. "Though I was but a boy, that does not pardon me. I am more sorry for it than anything I've ever done before or after that day."

The healer did not appear at all surprised. "I know, my son. Have always known."

He blinked. "How?"

"When you play cards with the devil, he tells you many things."

So, she still claimed that to be true? No matter. He did not come to Angus's chamber to pass judgment on what he did not understand but to apologize for what he'd done.

"He waits to claim me," Niall said, only partially jesting.

"Ahh, no. He knew you would be here now, attempting to atone for something you need not atone for. You were a boy, as you say, and held no real malice toward me."

"Nay," he agreed. "I did not then and do not now. Not toward you, mistress, only myself."

She looked at Angus. "Regret serves no purpose. Life is precarious, as you can see. But I do thank you for the apology."

Regret serves no purpose.

You held no real malice toward me.

Perhaps he should not so easily discount a woman who had saved many lives.

A knock at the door interrupted his thoughts.

Niall opened it, an awareness filling him. Lina. He wished to pull her toward him, hold her for all eternity. Instead, he let his wife inside.

"I've the herbs," she said, "and an apology from Glenhaven's healer who attends a birth at present. She will be here when the babe is born." Lina rushed to the healer's side.

"I've no need for her. These will work, or they will not. But we shall know Angus's fate soon enough.

He exchanged a glance with his wife as the healer went to work, grinding the herbs together.

Somehow, she knew why he was here. Her smile told him she approved, and Niall decided he could not wait a moment longer.

Taking Lina by the arm, he ushered her into the corridor. Cupping her face with both hands, he thought of the moment they met. And of how quickly his hate for her had turned to love, even if he'd not realized at the time.

Niall had much to tell her as they waited to learn Angus's fate, but he would not waste another moment of life without uttering the words he should have done so long ago.

"I love you, my lady wife," he said. "I've loved you for some time but did not know it, or knew it and was afraid to say as much lest you did not feel the same. I love your fire, your heart, your kindness, and most especially. . ." He could tell she thought he would say something about their lovemaking. Instead, he kissed her on the lips and pulled back. "Your aim."

She laughed. "That was not what I expected you to say."

"What do you expect then?" he asked.

His hands dropped down to her neck, gently caressing there, and then to the top of her shoulders where they remained, Niall wishing to feel the soft touch of his wife's skin.

"Something else," she said, still too shy to say the words.

No matter. He would teach her to say them, to tell him anything she wished. But for now, there was just one thing he wanted to know. And was about to ask when Lina blurted, "And I love you, Niall, as well you know."

"I did suspect," he teased, "but am glad to hear it."

He wanted to ask about the conversation she had with his father. Tell him of theirs. Talk of Angus and ask about the herbs. Tell her his thoughts on Kieran being his father's second. So much he wanted to tell his wife, but instead, he simply kissed her again.

They had a lifetime to discuss such things.

And would. 'Twould be he and Lina making a life together at Glenhaven Manor.

Together.

EPILOGUE

"You asked for a private meal so we could talk," Lina said as the serving girls left. They'd brought their suppers, as he requested, and the table in he and his wife's bedchamber was now laden with food.

"I did," he said, "and have matters I'd like to discuss. But that gown..."

Of all the ones she wore, it was that simple cream one with gold thread along the neckline and sleeves Niall loved most. She looked like an angel come from heaven even though he knew his wife had a very devilish side too. One he wished to explore this very moment.

Pulling her toward him, Niall spun her around and began to untie her gown. He was, in fact, quite proficient at it and removed the garment in quick order. She stepped out of it.

"The meal," he said, "will grow cold if you do not aid me. Your boots, my lady?"

Kneeling, he removed those as well. And her hose and garter. When Niall began to remove his own boots, Lina now in nothing but a shift, she offered a weak protest.

"Angus had that duck prepared especially for you, and now it will grow cold."

In the sennight since Angus had recovered, the man had not slowed his pace as Niall and others, including Lina, begged him to do. Instead, the steward completed the job of a man many years younger.

Thankful to remain alive, he said over and over. They were thankful for the same. Now, however, Niall was also thankful that his wife, despite her protests, was pulling her shift above her head.

No sooner were they both completely nude than Niall guided his wife to the bed. But she surprised him by stopping before they reached its edge, turning toward it. And didn't his wife sweep her hair to one side and bend over, placing both hands on the mattress. The sight of her bare buttocks, Lina in such a position...

They'd made love this way in the bed but never quite like this. Each time, however, his wife became more and more adventurous, though he should not have been surprised.

"Lina." His voice thick with desire, Niall reached between her legs thinking to prepare her for him, but 'twas unnecessary. She was so wet already, he pulled his fingers from her, grabbed her hip with one hand, and guided himself into her with the other.

He had to close his eyes or risk spilling his seed too soon. "Lord in heaven, wife."

She peered over her shoulder to look at him, the expression on her face one of pleasure mixed with merriment for Lina knew precisely what she did to him.

Buried fully in her, Niall remained there for a moment before pulling out. And then in. Reaching across her hip with his free hand, he rubbed her with his fingers, teasing and circling as she cried out his name.

He cried out hers.

Wanting it to last.

Wanting to remain inside his wife all eve. But he simply could not. The moment Lina's legs began to shake, her cries telling him she began to release, Niall immediately did the same, pushing himself as deep within her as possible.

He held himself there for some time, pulling away reluctantly.

Turning, his wife smiled in a way that told Niall she was quite pleased with herself for forcing him to nearly lose control. He pulled her into his arms.

"Mmmm, I did enjoy that, love."

"Did you?" she asked, looking up at him. "I was not certain."

He made another sound deep in his throat, kissed her, and would have remained that way for some time had there not been a knock at the door.

Knowing few would disturb them with Niall specifically asking to take his meal in private, he quickly dressed, at least partially, as Lina donned her shift once more.

He opened the door, revealing none other than Angus on the other side.

"Apologies, my lord. But your mother is belowstairs asking to see you."

"My mother?"

'Twas exceedingly odd, not that his mother had traveled to Glenhaven but arriving so late.

"I will send Mary," he said to Lina, following Angus from the chamber, "so that you may join us."

When they reached the hall, the evening meal was well

underway, with his own surely having grown cold abovestairs. His mother stood beside the fire, warming her hands.

He kissed her cheek in greeting. "Mother, is Father here with you?"

"He is not," she said. "It's he and your brother I came to speak to you about."

Niall did not understand. "Mother?" he asked, not caring for her expression. She seemed worried, much more so than usual. "They are well?"

"Indeed," she said, lowering her voice. "But I have a request to ask of you. And something to share you may find distressing. Though 'tis necessary."

Niall could not possibly be more confused. By his mother's sudden appearance. By her behavior. By her words. "What is your request?"

"I've learned you spoke to your father and brother about naming Kieran as second."

Ahh, now he understood.

"Aye," he said. "When Father refused to accept Lina, I'd suggested to Kieran I would be glad for him to be chief and I would serve him."

"You must not continue to suggest it."

Niall thought back to when he and Lina had last visited Castle Duncraig. "I may have reiterated my words once, to ensure Father knew I would, indeed, follow Kieran if ever such a thing were necessary."

"You are the chief's second, son."

His mother had never favored one of her sons before, and Niall thought it odd she would do so now.

"What is this, Mother? You come here and so late? To tell me not to encourage something that 'tis likely not to happen? Why?" And then he remembered. "You said you must tell me something that would be distressing?"

"What I will tell you is not something you can ever speak aloud to your father or brother." Though none could hear their conversation, despite that the hall was filled, his mother lowered her voice even more. "I would not have you keep it from your wife, but if she were to share the information with her brother..." His mother sighed. "I say this only because I know no other way than to ensure you do not press Kieran's suit as second."

"There is no suit," he reassured her again. "But aye, you've my confidence in anything you wish to tell me."

"Kieran," she said, and then stopped, looking around as if he would suddenly appear. "We took Kieran into our family when he'd not quite seen ten summers."

"All know this, Mother. But I do not believe any in our clan see Kieran as anything but your full son or as my full brother."

"Perhaps," she replied. "And some do know he came to be with us on the day after the Battle of The Black Friars."

That startled him. 'Twas something he did not know.

"Indeed?"

"Indeed," she said, still appearing worried. "But none, including your father or brother, who has long forgotten, know the precise circumstances."

"But why should it matter?" he asked, spotting Lina in the distance. His wife glided toward them.

"Because," she said. "Kieran could never be the chief of Clan Duncraig."

"Why?" he pressed. Clearly, the information his mother came to share was not any she comfortably wished to convey.

"Because your brother, Kieran, is a MacKinlay."

BE the first to read Kieran's story in *The Secret of Clan Duncraig*. Pre-order here on Amazon, coming October 2023.

BE the first to read a sneak peek of book two in the Highland Lovers duet—and get a free book—by becoming a CM Insider here.

ALSO BY CECELIA MECCA

Original Series

Border Series

Border Series Spin-Off

Brotherhood of the Border

Standalone Series

Order of the Broken Blade

ABOUT THE AUTHOR

Cecelia Mecca is the bestselling author of Scottish and medieval romance. Although the former English teacher's actual home is in Northeast Pennsylvania where she lives with her husband and two teens, her online home can be found at CeceliaMecca.com.

Printed in Great Britain
by Amazon